Mystery
on
Church Hill

By Steven K. Smith

MyBoys3 Press

MYSTERY
ON
CHURCH HILL

ONE

THE FIELD TRIP

T he line inched forward one millimeter at a time. Sam's stomach growled so loudly he thought everyone around him could hear it.

"What's taking so long?" he moaned.

He peered over the counter at the lunch ladies. With robot-like efficiency, they refilled shiny metal containers with stalks of green broccoli and a few hundred over-processed chicken nuggets. It looked kind of gross, but at this point Sam was so hungry, he'd eat just about anything.

Grrrowwllll his stomach cried out again.

He glanced up the line at Caitlin Murphy to see if she noticed. She had a smirk on her face like she knew something, but that was how she always looked, so he couldn't tell if it was because of him.

"Is that organic broccoli?" Caitlin asked one of the lunch ladies through a cloud of steam rising into the air.

Good grief.

Caitlin was always acting like she was too good for everything and smarter than everybody.

The lunch lady ignored her and turned to load more of what the school tried to pass off as food. Sam wasn't so sure it was. He suspected they mixed up dirt and sawdust in the kitchen and pretended it was nutritious. At least that's how it tasted most of the time.

"Let's move, Jackson!"

Sam felt a tray jab him in the back and looked over his shoulder. Billy Maxwell was about to run him over. The lunch line was moving again, and the hungry third graders were getting restless. Perhaps there would be a revolt.

Sam crept forward and held his tray out for the lunch lady to fill his plate. One of the steaming broccoli spears spilled off his tray and onto the floor. It rolled smack onto Caitlin's shoe.

"Eww!" she shrieked. "Sam Jackson, get your food *off* of me!"

"Sorry," said Sam. He reached down to grab the broccoli, but she kicked it across the floor before he could do anything.

"It's organic now, Caitlin!" laughed Billy.

Sam picked up a milk carton from the rack at the end

of the line and headed over to his class's third grade table. Lunch was already more than halfway over. His friends were almost finished with their lunches they'd brought from home. Sam sat at the end of the table and scarfed his food down.

The kids were raising a racket. The cafeteria grew louder and louder. Maybe it was the bad food. Or the weather. Ever since last week when the late February days were unseasonably warm, everyone seemed to be acting nuts. Sam's mom said the weather was giving all the kids "spring fever," whatever that was. Maybe if Sam went to the nurse she would give him some real food.

As Sam finished off his second chicken nugget, a voice blasted from the cafeteria PA system. "Third grade! QUIET DOWN!"

It was Ms. Saltwater, the cafeteria monitor. She ruled the cafeteria with an iron fist, the microphone being her weapon of choice.

"It is entirely too LOUD in here, students!"

Since she talked with the microphone so close to her mouth, it sounded more like "RAH RAH RAHHH!"

Sam thought the mic might actually be *in* her mouth. Maybe she had swallowed it and sounded like that even when she was away from school. He shuddered just thinking about running into Ms. Saltwater in town. Her name was actually Ms. Salwalter, but everyone called her 'Saltwater' because she was so mean.

Like a shark.

Maybe she'd eaten too many of the chicken nuggets – or a kid.

The third grade did not quiet down enough to please Ms. Saltwater. Everyone had to finish their lunch period with their heads down on the tables while she walked up and down the aisles like a prison guard. She swung the microphone back and forth in her hands like one of those batons used for beating people.

Sam peeked up from his arms once when she walked by and he swore she was growling. Brandon was making faces at him from across the table until Ms. Saltwater came up behind him, smacking her hand down on the lunch table.

Bang!

"QUIET!" she yelled.

Yikes.

Eventually the bell rang. Much to Ms. Saltwater's disappointment, the students were released to their classrooms. When Sam's class got back to their desks, his teacher, Mrs. Haperwink, had written something on the whiteboard in big block letters.

"RICHMOND'S HISTORY."

Before she could begin speaking, a hand went up in the back of the room. It was Billy Maxwell.

"Yes, Billy, what is it? I haven't even asked a question yet."

"Are we all going to die?" he shouted.

Everyone burst out laughing.

Billy gave a high five to Brandon Perth who was sitting next to him like they'd just scored a goal.

"Billy, what on earth are you talking about?" Mrs. Haperwink sighed.

"Well, the board says 'Richmond's History,' so I figured we'll all be goners since we live in Richmond!"

More laughter ensued. Brandon clutched his stomach and acted like he was going to roll out of his seat. Mrs. Haperwink, whom everyone but Caitlin called 'Mrs. H,' looked exasperated. She glanced up at the clock like she was counting the minutes left until summer vacation.

In the seat next to Sam, Caitlin raised her hand until Mrs. H gave her a weary nod. "Mrs. Haperwink, are we going to talk about our field trip now? I've been reading about Richmond's history online and in the book I checked out of the library. I'm *very* excited to learn more about it on our trip."

"Thank you, Caitlin, for being so interested in what we're learning," beamed Mrs. H.

Caitlin turned around and gave Billy a look. It was the same one that she'd given Sam in the lunch line.

"Tomorrow," the teacher continued, "we will be visiting St. John's Church in the historic Church Hill section of Richmond. Can anyone tell me what is so special about Church Hill?"

"There's a church there?" shouted Tommy Banks to a shower of chuckles from the class.

Caitlin's hand shot up once again. Thankfully Mrs. H ignored it this time. Sam didn't know if he could bear to hear her superior voice give yet another snotty answer today. He tried to think about the question. For some reason St. John's Church sounded very familiar to him, but he couldn't remember why.

"I'll give you a hint, boys and girls. It has to do with a very famous speech given around the time of the American Revolution."

Sam's thoughts came together all at once. That's it! He raised his hand.

"Sam, do you know the answer?" Mrs. H asked, sounding a bit surprised. Sam and his family had just moved to Virginia the previous summer. As a result, he hadn't learned as much about the local history and places as the rest of the class.

Caitlin squirmed in her seat. She raised her hand higher, not wanting to miss out on the opportunity to show off more of her knowledge.

Sam cleared his throat. "That's where Patrick Henry gave his speech about liberty." Out of the corner of his eye he saw Caitlin lower her hand and sink into her seat like a deflated balloon. "He said, 'Give me liberty or give me death!'"

"See – death! We're all going to die!" Billy yelled

again. "We're doomed!" The class busted out laughing again.

"Out in the hallway, Billy!" Mrs. H ordered. "NOW!"

Billy sauntered out of the room with his head held high like he had won the jackpot. Caitlin stuck her tongue out at him as he walked by her desk. Sam just shook his head.

Billy was funny sometimes, but he always went too far. It was just like Sam's older brother, Derek, who was almost eleven and down the hall in fourth grade. He always tried to be a comedian and thought he was God's gift to the world.

Mrs. H turned back to Sam. "That's correct, Sam. Very impressive! Patrick Henry delivered a passionate plea for Virginia to provide troops for the American Revolution against England. It took place during the Second Virginia Convention in 1775. They met in St. John's Church, because at the time it was the only building in Richmond big enough to hold everyone.

"Tomorrow we will take buses to the church, and there may even be a short reenactment of that famous speech. I'd like everyone to read the chapter in your textbook about the revolution, beginning on page 249. To make our trip more meaningful, you'll want to know about several other important people and events that started the revolution."

Sam thought back to why he remembered Patrick Henry. Right after his family moved to Virginia from up north last summer, he and Derek made an amazing discovery. They found an old coin collection that had been stolen from the Virginia museum sixty years earlier. Some of the rarest and most valuable coins were the 1877 Indian Head cents. Since they had a picture of Lady Liberty wearing a feather headdress, it had reminded their mom of Patrick Henry's famous liberty speech given nearby.

Maybe some history does come in handy, decided Sam, as Mrs. H went over the details of the trip. Most of the history they learned in school seemed so boring, but it might be pretty cool to see the actual place where Patrick Henry gave his speech.

* * *

AS THEY GOT off the bus that afternoon, Sam told Derek about the plans for his class trip the next day.

"No way!" said his brother. "That sounds cool. I wonder if Patrick Henry's ghost haunts the place."

"I don't think he was buried there, Derek. It's just where he gave the speech."

"Well, keep a look out for his ghost just in case. It's an old church, and you know what they have at old churches."

Derek looked at Sam with a spooky grin.

"What? What do they have at old churches?" Sam couldn't help asking.

Derek leaned into Sam's face, opening his eyes wide. "Graveyards," he whispered, followed by a loud "Boo!"

Sam jumped and Derek ran down the driveway, laughing like a maniac all the way to their house where Mom was waiting on the porch.

Even though Sam knew Derek was just messing with him, he didn't like talking about ghosts or graveyards. They scared him. He tried to think about Patrick Henry giving his speech and not about whether he was now a ghost. He was thankful the field trip was during the daytime. Nothing creepy could happen then.

TWO

THE GRAVEYARD

The two yellow school buses chugged up the steep hill, coming to an idle next to the curb. Sam and the rest of his class filed out onto the sidewalk and looked around.

A black wrought-iron fence lined both corners of the block like the edges of a triangle. The fence had sharp decorative points along the top that looked like spears. The kind that always seemed to be waiting to impale someone. Sam imagined trying to climb the iron bars and accidentally slipping and falling onto one of the points and watching his guts spill out. That wouldn't be good.

Below the fence were rows of crusty red bricks. Like everything else he could see, they looked extremely old. That makes sense, thought Sam, since it was back in the 1700s when Patrick Henry spoke here. He peered through the iron bars and up the hill. A stately white steeple poked up from behind a tree. That must be St. John's Church. He eyed the grounds around the church and gulped. They were littered with faded, crooked headstones and tall gray concrete and marble monuments.

It was a cemetery.

"Great," muttered Sam.

"Hey, Jackson!" Billy walked up behind Sam. "You know why they have this fence around the graveyard?"

"No, why?"

"Because people are dying to get in! Hahaha!" laughed Billy.

Sam rolled his eyes.

"Get it, they're *dying* to get in! It's a cemetery!"

"Yeah, I get it. That's hilarious," Sam said in a voice that made it clear he didn't think it was very hilarious.

Mrs. H marched the kids up the steps to the cemetery entrance. They stood in the groups of threes that she had constructed. Somehow Sam had been stuck with both Billy and Caitlin. Definitely not a match made in heaven, as his mom would say. He wasn't sure what was the worst – Billy's jokes, Caitlin's snobbery, or the cemetery. He tried not to look at the tombstones in the grass all around him, but he couldn't help it. Caitlin was acting like a tour guide and kept blabbing about every detail that they passed.

"Look, this person was born in 1723. This one in 1747. Wow – 1711!"

"We get it," said Sam, trying to keep his eyes on the sidewalk. "They're old."

"Hey, Caitlin, ya know why they have fences around graveyards?"

"Shut up, Billy," she retorted and walked around to the back of another big stone monument.

Before Billy could give a comeback, Caitlin shouted to them. "Look at this one, he was a signer of the Declaration of Independence. That is *so* amazing!"

"What would be amazing," said Billy, "is if Mrs. H gave Sam and me *our* independence and moved you out of our group, Caitlin."

This was going to be a long day.

Sam walked up to the gravestone to see what Caitlin was carrying on about. He was still getting used to seeing so many historical things all over the place in Virginia. It was pretty cool that the tombstones were so ancient. Not *ancient* ancient, like the pyramids in Egypt or the Coliseum in Rome. But they were ancient for America.

"George Wythe," Sam read on the stone. He pronounced the last name with a long 'Y' like '*eye*.' "Did he really sign the Declaration of Independence?"

Caitlin wriggled her nose. "Yes, he did. And his name is pronounced 'with,' Sam. Like, I can't believe that I have to be *with* Billy all day on this field trip."

It wasn't enough that Caitlin knew who this guy was. Of course she had to know how to pronounce his name correctly as well. Caitlin would take any chance she could to act smart.

Sam didn't want to encourage her, but he couldn't help being curious. "Okay, but didn't our book say that Thomas Jefferson wrote the Declaration of Independence?"

Caitlin gave him another look like she couldn't believe he didn't already know the answer. "Thomas Jefferson wrote it, but all the members of the Continental Congress signed it. Including George W-y-the," she explained, dragging out Wythe's last name. "It rhymes with Smith."

Mrs. H called all the groups over to the church entrance. A tour guide wearing funny-looking clothes from colonial times stepped in front of them. Sam looked him over and was immediately grateful not to have lived back then.

The man had navy blue pants that just barely covered his knees with tall white socks that reminded Sam of a baseball uniform. He wore a yellow vest and a white shirt underneath. It was tied tightly around his neck and had strange ruffly cuffs on his wrists. On top he wore a dark blue coat with lots of gold buttons. Judging by the way he was sweating, the outfit must have been really hot.

The tour guide wore a white wig over his real hair with a ponytail down the back tied in a big bow. It reminded Sam of pictures he'd seen of George Washington, but he'd never thought about George Washington looking so weird.

The oddly dressed tour guide led them through the doors of the old church. The first thing Sam noticed were rows and rows of dark wooden benches. Each bench had a high back separating it from the one behind it. Halfway down the bench was a divider, sectioning them like booths at a restaurant without any tables in the middle. On the end of each row there was a door. When it was shut, the pew looked like a rectangular box.

Sam imagined sitting on the benches for church on Sunday. There weren't any seat cushions, and the backs were angled straight up. He couldn't decide which looked more uncomfortable – the seats or the clothes. Dealing with both at the same time must have been horrible!

The tour guide launched into the full history of St. John's Church, starting with its construction way back in 1741. The class followed him through the aisles to the spot where historians believed Patrick Henry stood when he delivered his 'Give me liberty or give me death' speech. The guide rambled on for what seemed like an hour about why the speech was so important.

Sam stopped listening to the tour guide somewhere around his description of the Second Continental Congress. He was sure it was all very important, but he really needed to use the bathroom. The ride on the bus hadn't been that long, but Billy had brought a giant-sized bottle of sports drink. Unfortunately, Sam had drunk a little too much. There was something about that lemon-lime flavor that made him have to pee like a racehorse.

Sam found his way over to Mrs. H in the back of the group. When he told her his dilemma, she pointed at the side door and whispered for him to come straight back.

Sam found a sign pointing to the left that said 'Restrooms' and headed in that direction. He went through a side door and found himself back outside again. A hodgepodge of gravestones and outbuildings were set on a slope around the church. The black impaling fence surrounded him in all directions.

One building had a sign that read *Gift Shop*. Like everything else, it was made of bricks and dripped of oldness. It had a few signs and shirts for sale in the window. A couple of them said, 'If this be treason, make the most of it – Patrick Henry 1765.' Sam wasn't sure what that meant. He'd have to ask Mrs. H later.

Patrick Henry seemed to be kind of a loudmouth.

He reminded Sam of Caitlin.

Sam walked down the slope and around the corner of the church. He saw a large metal door to what looked like the basement. It was slightly ajar with an unlocked padlock hanging from the doorframe. He hoped this was the way to the bathroom. It didn't really look like it, but the sign had pointed this way and he didn't see anything else.

He reached out and gave the door a tug. It opened with a dim hallway stretching ahead of him. The walls were made of rough stone and a single light bulb hung from a wire on the ceiling.

"This can't be right," mumbled Sam. But he really had to go, so he moved into the hallway. Maybe bathrooms were always in dark basement hallways during colonial times.

Sam wandered through the dark corridor, keeping a hand on the wall to maintain his balance. The stone floor was uneven, and he caught his toe on a couple of rocks that were sticking up in his path. He was about to give up and turn around when he heard something up ahead. He stopped in his tracks, thinking about Patrick Henry's ghost. He listened carefully and heard a man's voice coming from around the bend.

"Are you sure you hit the right spot? I don't see anything," the voice said.

Another man answered. "Yeah, it's right here. I walked it off exactly from upstairs. This wall is right underneath the…what was that crazy phrase?"

"Underneath the one who spoke of liberty," said the other man.

"Right – that one. But there's nothing here. Measure it yourself if you don't trust me."

"If Jerry thinks we messed this up, we'll be dead meat."

"Maybe this Sweeney guy didn't know what he was talking about. Where'd Jerry find that diary, anyway? Up in his attic or something? All that gibberish about the marker. Blah, blah! If I wanted a history lesson, I would've gone to college. This church is, like, 200 years old. Who knows what could have happened during that time?"

Sam pushed his body against the stone wall, afraid to move a muscle. This definitely wasn't the way to the bathroom. He knew he should get out of there, but he was curious to know what these guys were talking about. He didn't recognize the names "Sweeney" or "Jerry." Did something else happen here 200 years ago besides Patrick Henry's speech?

The man started talking again. "Listen, all that stuff is Jerry's job, not ours. He's the fancy historian. We're just supposed to dig." Then the sound of metal against stone echoed down the hall.

Sam took two small steps forward. He leaned around the corner to get a look at the men. They had their backs to him and were working with a crowbar to pry some old stones out of the wall.

This was getting too weird. Sam turned to sneak out. Instead, he smacked hard into a wall and nearly fell over. At least it had felt like a wall. Sam looked up and saw it was actually a man – a big one.

"Where do you think you're going, kid?" the tall man snarled.

Sam couldn't see him very well in the shadowy hallway, but this wasn't one of the men he'd been watching. Sam's cheek ached. He must have smashed his face into one of the big gold buttons on the man's jacket.

"I, uh…" stuttered Sam. "I was looking for the bathroom, but I think I'm lost."

"What are you looking at in there?" The man stepped back closer to the light bulb. He was dressed in one of the colonial costumes, just like their tour guide.

This guy must work here. He'd know what to do, thought Sam. "There's two men back there digging in the wall. They kind of look like they might be stealing something," Sam explained in a low voice.

"Two guys, huh? Let's go check it out."

Sam turned to leave using the door he'd come in by. He'd seen more than enough for one day. Mrs. H was probably wondering where he'd gone by now. He took a step forward, but the man grabbed his shirt with a jerk.

"Not so fast, kid. You're coming too."

Sam's body tensed. He started sweating as the big man pulled him down the passageway.

"No, really, I've seen enough," Sam cried. He tried to pull away, but his feet were lifted right off the ground. The man seemed to be as strong as a linebacker. They turned the corner and came up behind the other men.

"Making enough noise, you idiots?" yelled the tall man. "You were supposed to be out of here already. There are tours up there!"

Sam felt dizzy. This guy was with the other two? He shouldn't have come down here. What were they going to do to him?

"Who's the kid, Jerry?"

"He was watching you from the hallway. He saw everything, didn't you, kid?" the tall man named Jerry asked.

"No, really! I, I didn't see anything," Sam stammered. "I'm just trying to find the bathroom. I need to get back to my class. Really. I gotta go."

"We'll see about that." Jerry shoved Sam against the wall.

Sam's heart felt like it was about to explode out of his chest. Would Mrs. H hear him if he screamed as loud as he could?

Jerry turned and looked at the hole the other men had dug. "Well, where is it?"

"There's nothing here, Jerry. We followed the directions you told us exactly. Nada. That Sweeney guy must have it wrong."

Jerry smacked the man on the head. "What's the matter with you? Don't use any names in front of the kid!" He turned and glared at Sam.

Sam felt like he was going to puke. This couldn't be

happening. He bent over and stared down at his feet. There was a baseball-sized rock against the wall next to him. When he glanced up, the men were all staring at the hole in the wall on the other side of the small room. No one was looking at him.

Almost without thinking, Sam reached down and picked up the rock. He heaved it at the big man in front of him. Since Jerry was so close, Sam's only choice was to aim for his legs. The rock hit Jerry square in the side of the kneecap, bouncing off with a thud.

"Ahh!" the man screamed, falling onto his other knee.

"What the…" One of the other guys whirled around to see what was going on.

Sam bounced off the crouched man's shoulder and headed for the hallway. He didn't look back at the men.

He just ran.

THREE

THE CHURCH

Sam flung open the basement door and exploded out
into the sunlight. He looked left and right but he
didn't see his class anywhere. The grounds were empty
except for the tombstones poking out of the grass. Sam
ran around the corner and bounded through the side
door into the church. He nearly toppled into Caitlin and
Billy, who were bickering in the aisle.

"Billy, that is disgusting!" yelled Caitlin. The look on
her face suggested that Billy had just said something
gross, which wasn't all that unusual. Sam bent over in
front of them, hands on his knees, gasping for breath.

"Where's the fire, Jackson?" asked Billy.

"Quick!" Sam panted, scanning the room. "We have
to hide!"

"Sam, where have you been?" scolded Caitlin. "Mrs.
Haperwink sent us looking for you. We're wasting time

that we could be spending in the gift shop. We're supposed to meet everyone there and—"

"No time to explain…Come on…They're going to get me!" Sam grabbed her arm and hurried down the aisle to the middle of the church.

"Ouch! Sam, that hurts! What's wrong?" Caitlin said.

"Come on, get down!" whispered Sam. "I'm not joking, we have to hide!" He opened one of the big wooden doors at the end of the rows and scurried under the bench. He pulled Caitlin in behind him, motioning for Billy to follow.

"Man, Jackson, I think you've blown a gasket!" Billy said, chuckling. "But if this means we don't have to go back to school, I'm with you, brother!"

Billy climbed under the bench, squeezing up tight with the others. Sam leaned out and pulled the door shut with a bang.

"You know," whispered Billy, leaning closer to Caitlin, "it's kind of spooky in here!" He made a sound that echoed like a ghost.

Caitlin scowled at Billy in the dark cramped space.

"Shhh!" hissed Sam. "Be quiet!"

Before they could argue further, a loud creak of the wooden church door rang through the room. Sam inched his head up and saw the three men from the basement charge in. He ducked back down to stay out of sight.

"Do you see him?" yelled one of the men.

Sam crouched lower into the shadow of the bench and put his finger to his lips. Billy and Caitlin's eyes opened wider when they heard the men's voices.

"You guys are so stupid," growled a deep voice that Sam recognized as Jerry's. "If you'd have just done your job right in the first place, this wouldn't have happened."

"It's just a little kid, Jerry, what are you worried about?" said one of the diggers.

"Yeah, he doesn't know anything," added the other man.

"Shut up and look down the aisles," Jerry said.

Under the pew bench, the kids could hear footsteps moving slowly down the wooden floorboards. Two of the men made quiet steps, but one walked with a loud clackety-clack. Sam figured that was Jerry's shoes from his colonial costume.

The clackety-clack footsteps stopped near their row.

Everything was dead silent.

Sam could barely make out Caitlin's face in the dark, but she looked scared.

Just as it seemed like the man would never leave, the clackety-clack started up again as he moved to the back of the church.

"Forget it. The little creep must have left with his group. Let's get out of here," Jerry ordered. "You two get back down there. Clean up that mess before we have any more surprises. And this time, lock that door like I told you!"

"Okay, Jerry, no problem. Take it easy."

"I'll take it easy when this is done. I'm taking a big risk here. And make sure you smooth out the dirt behind the marker too. I don't want anybody nosing around here and getting suspicious." The voices faded as the men skulked back outside. The door banged shut behind them.

Sam was sure he could hear his heart pounding through the silence. Billy was starting to squirm next to him, but Sam waited ten more seconds before slowly peeking his head over the bench.

The church was quiet. The men were gone.

A shrill squeak broke the silence.

"Eww! Billy!" shouted Caitlin, holding her nose. She jumped up from their hiding spot and smacked Billy in the shoulder. "Don't *ever* do that again!"

"We were sitting under there a long time!" Billy explained through a wide grin and turned to Sam. "That was epic!"

Sam finally exhaled a long breath and stood up. "Knock it off, you guys!"

Caitlin moved into the aisle and watched the door. "Sam, who were those men?" she asked. "Were they looking for you? What have you been doing?"

"Yeah, I ran into them when I was looking for the

bathroom. They were searching for something in the basement, and they grabbed me." Sam shuddered as he remembered feeling the tall man clutch his shoulders.

Billy slapped Sam on the back. "Whoa, Jackson, you were almost history!"

Sam quietly led the way to the front of the church, opening the door just enough to see through the crack. "Come on, let's get out of here. We can talk about it on the bus." He motioned them forward into the cemetery.

* * *

THE BUS BOUNCED over a pothole as it sped down Church Hill. Sam turned his head and saw the steeple of St. John's Church disappear behind some trees in the distance. That was one class trip he would not soon forget.

He realized he'd never gone to the bathroom. With all of the excitement, he didn't need to go anymore. He hoped his eyeballs didn't turn yellow.

Caitlin looked over at Sam. "So what was that all about?" She was next to him in a three-seater.

Billy leaned over from the seat in front of them. Caitlin had refused to let him in their row, so he had to sit next to Janice Sweetsen, who always smelled like oranges. Janice claimed it was because she was so sweet, but Sam didn't think so. Caitlin said maybe some of it would rub off on Billy.

Sam glanced over the seat toward the front of the bus. "Keep your voice down. I don't want Mrs. H to hear us." Their teacher was showing one of the class moms a package of homemade colonial soap she'd bought in the gift shop.

Sam quietly recounted his escapades in the basement to Billy and Caitlin.

"Holy cow!" yelled Billy, loud enough for the entire bus to hear. Everybody turned and stared at them. Sam gave Billy a fierce scowl.

Mrs. H looked up from her soap. "Billy, turn around in your seat!"

"Do you even know what 'inconspicuous' means, Billy?" asked Caitlin.

Billy sat down, but he jammed his head into the crack between the seat cushion and the window so he could still hear. "What are you going to do?" he tried to whisper.

"What could they have been searching for?" Caitlin asked.

"Well, we know one thing," said Sam. "They said, 'beneath the one that spoke of liberty' – that's got to be Patrick Henry, right? It's why St. John's Church is so famous."

"So something important is underneath the spot where Patrick Henry gave his speech?" asked Caitlin.

"I guess," said Sam. "They were digging for something in the stone wall, but nothing was there. They were worried the tall guy, Jerry, would be mad at them."

"What did they mean when they talked in the church about covering something up by the marker?" asked Caitlin. "What's a marker?"

"Maybe they stole a magic marker from some kid on a tour and they wanted to hide the evidence," said Billy from behind the seat.

Sam remembered hearing about markers before. "I think a marker can be another name for a gravestone."

They all sat silently, listening to the bus motoring along the highway.

"Maybe it was a Sharpie," said Billy, breaking the quiet. "You have to be careful what you write on with those."

Caitlin glared at him.

"What?" asked Billy. "The ink doesn't come out if you get it on your clothes. My mom hates that."

Sam rolled his eyes and tried to focus. "This is complicated," he said. "I think we need to do more research. They said it was 200 years old and mentioned someone else named Sweeney. I didn't hear anything about someone named Sweeney on the tour, did you?"

"No, I didn't," said Caitlin. She pulled her notebook

out of her bag. "I think we need to make a list of what we don't know."

Caitlin was just too organized sometimes, thought Sam. On the paper she wrote:

Questions:

1. *Spoke on liberty = Patrick Henry*
2. *What is underneath him?*
3. *Who is Sweeney?*
4. *What happened 200 years ago?*
5. *What is a marker?*

"I told you, it's a Sharpie," said Billy, straining to see.

"Billy, please!" Caitlin copied the list onto a second piece of paper and gave it to Sam. "I can try to do some digging on the computer to find more answers."

"And I'll talk to my brother, Derek," said Sam. "He loves mysteries, and I think we've definitely found another one!"

FOUR

THE PLAN

S am got a ride home from school with Michael
   Harmon's mom since their class returned from the
field trip after the normal bus dismissal. When he got
back to his house, Sam threw his backpack against the
wall and dashed upstairs to his bedroom that he shared
with Derek. He found his brother standing on his bed
with headphones on, bopping to a song on his iPod.

"Derek!"

Derek turned around and smiled. He gave Sam the
thumbs up sign. Then he started to wiggle his arms back
and forth like he was a wave on the ocean.

"Derek!" Sam called again. He reached up and
yanked at the ear buds.

"Hey! I was just getting to the good part," Derek said.
"You were about to see my signature move."

He jumped off the bed and struck a pose toward his

reflection in the mirror like he was really hot stuff. Ever since they started at their new school this year after finding the lost coins, Derek considered himself a bit of a local celebrity. Sam figured it would wear off eventually, but he hoped it would be soon.

"Knock it off and listen to me!" yelled Sam. "You're not going to believe this. I think I've found another mystery!"

"No way, did you find more coins?" asked Derek. "I thought they searched the woods and didn't find anything last summer."

"Not coins – this could be even better," Sam said. "Do you remember how Mom told us about that speech Patrick Henry gave?"

Derek looked back at the mirror, standing straight as an arrow. He dramatically held his arm out and sang in an opera-singer voice, "Give me liberty, or give me death!" He stumbled backward and collapsed on the bed.

"Bravo, Derek. Now stop it and listen," Sam said. "You know how I had my field trip at St. John's?"

"Yeah. Wait, don't tell me." Derek put his hand on his forehead and closed his eyes like he was doing a magic trick. "I see a church…and a hill…?"

Sam sighed. Why did Derek always have to be such a screwball?

"Yes, but you won't believe what happened *at* the church," Sam said. He sat on the edge of the bed and told

Derek everything. He read back the list Caitlin had written on the bus.

"We should go back there and look around," said Derek. "The only way to answer these questions is to get more clues."

"Uh, no way!" said Sam.

"What do you mean, no?" asked Derek. "Why not?"

Sam stood up and paced. "Well, for one thing, I was just there. And for another, did you not hear me say those guys nearly killed me?"

"They weren't going to kill you – I'll bet you just surprised them. What we need," Derek said, "is a good excuse for Mom and Dad to take us back there. We can't wait for the next class trip to roll around. They'd like all the history. Mom's really into that kind of stuff, isn't she?"

"I don't think you're hearing me," said Sam. He stopped his pacing to look Derek in the eye.

"Sam, if we quit every time you got scared, we'd just sit in our room all day. We need to get out there and solve this mystery! Now help me think. How can we get Mom and Dad there?"

Sam closed his eyes. There was no use fighting Derek once he got started on these crazy ideas. "Well, our tour guide said there's a special reenactment program this Sunday afternoon."

"Really? That's perfect!" Derek leaped up, smiling.

"Perfect for you. Derek, I really don't want to see those guys again. It makes me ill just thinking about it."

"They're probably long gone by now," said Derek. "And we'll be there with Mom and Dad. No one is going to try to hurt us if we're with them."

"That depends on how bad these guys are," said Sam. "What if they're murderers? What if they're hired assassins for a South American drug lord? What if they kill people for fun, just to watch them die?"

"You've been watching too many movies," said Derek, laughing.

Sam sat for a minute, thinking about Derek's plan. He *did* have a tendency to get overly anxious. But Derek usually took things too far.

"Maybe you're right," Sam said. "They did seem more like thieves than killers."

"Great, then we'll go to the reenactment. It'll be our cover. We'll bring Mom and Dad for safety, and while we're there, we can look for more clues. Now let's go talk Mom into it."

Derek marched out of the room before Sam could argue further. Sam followed him downstairs and watched Derek ambush their mom in the kitchen.

"Mom, we have to go back to St. John's Church!" Derek blurted out.

"We do?" Mom was stirring something over the stove. "Did Sam leave something there?"

"No, but he told me about his field trip. It sounded awesome! That place is filled with history. I know that you and Dad would really enjoy the educational value Sam and I could get from seeing it all again."

"Excuse me?" Mom laughed. "I think you must be in the wrong house. Educational value? Who are you, and what have you done with my son?"

"Our tour guide said they have reenactments of Patrick Henry giving his famous speech," joined in Sam. "Remember how you told us about that?"

"Didn't you study history in college?" asked Derek. "You'd love it! I'm thinking about writing a paper for extra credit for Mrs. Lincolnmuller."

"Oh, honey, you must be sick!" said Mom. "Come here. Let me feel your forehead."

"It's true, Mom," said Sam. "We should go." He didn't sound quite as enthusiastic as Derek, but he was trying to play along.

"Oh, no, it must be contagious!" said Mom. "You've caught it too!"

"Very funny, Mom," said Sam. "Can we go on Sunday? They're having a program and it's not far."

"Well, if you're really serious, it does sound fascinating," said Mom, getting back to the stove. "I was excited to hear that your class was going there in the first place. Let me talk to Dad and see what he thinks."

"All right!" Derek gave Sam a toothy grin. Sam

weakly tapped Derek's outstretched hand for a high-five as they left the room. He had a sneaking suspicion this wasn't such a great idea at all.

* * *

THE MORNING OF THE REENACTMENT, sunlight streamed through the kitchen window. It reflected off a spoon on the breakfast table with a blinding light. Dozens of sparkling reflections danced off the far wall like a movie projector. Sam watched them glisten for a few seconds and then pulled the curtain across to block the rays while he ate.

He hadn't slept well. He lay in bed for a long time thinking about Church Hill. He must be crazy to go back there. He splashed milk over the bananas and Chee-rios in his bowl. It formed white waterfalls over the round pieces of cereal that floated like miniature life preservers.

Derek wandered into the kitchen and plopped down into his chair with a thud. "Who won the game last night?"

"I don't know. I can't find Mom's phone. Try the paper." Sam crunched between bites. "Maybe Dad brought it in before he left for the gym."

Derek walked over to the counter and picked up a banana. He grabbed the newspaper from under a box of cinnamon muffins and pulled out the sports section. He dumped the rest of the paper on the table next to Sam.

"Guess who won?" he said, flipping through the pages. "It's worth two points."

Sam didn't answer. He didn't feel like playing Derek's game. They were always competing over something, even when it didn't matter. Dad had started it when they were little by telling them they'd get "points" when he wanted them to do something. The boys had carried on the tradition themselves, even though the points never counted for anything. Sam suspected Derek secretly kept an ongoing tally of who was leading, just so he could win. But Sam was too tired for the game this morning. Derek could have all the points he wanted.

Derek moved his finger up and down the page, pointing at the lines of box scores. "All right, the Rams won! 68-52! Look at this awesome dunk picture!"

Sam leaned out of his seat to see the page, his curiosity to see a cool dunk overtaking his drowsiness. As he stretched across the table, he knocked over a half-full glass of orange juice. It quickly spread across the surface to the rest of the newspaper.

"Sam!"

"Whoops, sorry."

"Don't just say sorry! Get something to mop it up!" shouted Derek.

"All right, all right," Sam said with a huff. He grabbed

a wad of napkins and blotted up the wet pieces of newspaper. He was starting to pick them up when something caught his eye on the front page of the Metro section.

He froze in mid-wipe.

The juice found the crack in the middle of the table and began dripping onto the wooden floor.

"Hey, Earth to Sam!" Derek hollered when he noticed Sam not cleaning up the mess. "What's the matter with you? What are you looking at?"

"It's him!" Sam whispered, pointing to a photo that had mostly escaped the flood of orange juice. The picture showed a group of strangely dressed men standing in front of a big white building.

"It's who?" said Derek. "What's that picture?"

"It's the guy from St. John's Church, the guy I ran into in the basement! It's *him*, Jerry!"

"What? No way! Are you sure?"

Derek read the caption under the picture on the page:

Participants prepare for historic reenactment at St. John's Church, Sunday at 2 PM.

"You mean the guy who tried to grab you was one of the reenactment people dressed up in colonial costumes?" asked Derek.

"Yeah, did I leave that part out yesterday?"

"Yes, I think you failed to mention that part," said Derek. "Why would someone in the reenactment try to grab a kid? That doesn't make any sense."

"It does make sense. He was trying to steal something out of that wall in the basement, and I interrupted him."

Sam pulled the edge of the curtain back and scanned the yard. "Change of plans. We can't go back to the church if he's *definitely* going to be there. He'll see me for sure!"

"I'll tell you what," Derek said in his most confident voice. "We'll put you in a disguise so he won't recognize you. Is this place big? You can blend right in. He'll never know you're there."

"Yeah, it's pretty big," said Sam. "There are lots of rows of benches."

"Perfect," said Derek, smiling. "We'll sit in the back during the performance. When it's over and the actors are off signing autographs or something, we'll take a better look around."

"I don't think they're the kind of actors that sign autographs, Derek. It's not Hollywood, it's a historical reenactment."

"Okay, well, we'll figure something out. Don't worry – it's going to be fun. I'm ready for another great mystery to solve. If it works out as well as the last one did, we'll be golden!"

"Or we could be dead," Sam said with a groan. "That would be worse."

THE REENACTMENT

"Boys, come on!" called Dad. "The program's going to start soon and we need to get a seat. You don't want to sit in the back row, do you?"

Sam and Derek followed behind their parents up the sidewalk that led into St. John's Church.

"That's exactly what I want to do," grumbled Sam.

"We'll be there in a second," shouted Derek. "You guys go ahead and get some seats. Sam wants to show me one of these cool old gravestones."

"Okay, but it starts in five minutes," said Mom. "And Sam, take off that silly looking hat. This is a church after all." She walked in the front door, shaking her head.

Derek looked over at Sam. He was hiding under the shadow of a tree just off the sidewalk between two tombstones.

"I look ridiculous," said Sam.

"You said you wanted a disguise. You look good!"
Derek let out a little chuckle. Sam was wearing an over-
sized hat they'd found in the back of their dad's closet
with dark sunglasses that kept slipping down his nose.

"I need a disguise from my disguise," muttered Sam.

"Don't worry about it, you're not going on a date!"
said Derek. "Now let's look at these gravestones before
things start. We need to figure out what marker those
guys were talking about. Are there any special graves? Any
famous people buried here?"

"The tour guide said a couple of Virginia governors'
graves are here, and the mother of some guy named Poe.
Oh, wait." Sam remembered the grave he'd seen with
Billy and Caitlin. "There was one more grave, and it was
important. It's over here."

Sam led Derek over to the edge of the sidewalk to a
large stone.

"George Wythe...." read Derek, pronouncing the last
name as Sam had earlier, like the letter 'Y'.

"With," said Sam.

"With who?"

"No, his name – With." Sam could hear Caitlin's
voice in his head correcting him.

"What's with whose name?" said Derek.

Sam smacked his hand to his forehead. He felt like he
was in that old black-and-white comedy Dad had showed
him where two guys were arguing about the names of

baseball players. "No, you pronounce it 'Wi-th.' It rhymes with Smith."

"Ohhh," said Derek. "Why didn't you say so?"

"I did!" shouted Sam.

"Okay then," said Derek, "so George Y-th, With, whatever. Who is he? I mean, who was he?"

"You can read, can't you?" With a sigh, Sam pointed at the large plaque on the enormous gray stone. It listed the key accomplishments of the late Mr. Wythe.

"Wow," said Derek, reading the plaque. "So he was really a signer of the Declaration of Independence? That's pretty cool. If a marker means a gravestone, do you think this is the one those men were talking about?"

"It could be. I think it would be from around the same time when Patrick Henry gave his speech."

"Hey, look here on the plaque," said Derek. "It says Wythe taught Randolph, Jefferson and Marshall. Is that Thomas Jefferson? I don't know who those other names are."

"I think so," answered Sam.

"Well, that's pretty cool if he was Thomas Jefferson's teacher. He was an important dude all right!"

The church bell began to ring. Two old men hurried past them up the sidewalk to the entrance.

"I think the reenactment is about to begin, Derek." Sam turned. His brother was kneeling behind the stone, peering down at the dirt.

"What are you doing?" Sam hissed. "You can't dig up his bones!"

"Listen…I think I hear something." Derek put his ear to the ground in front of the stone.

"What is it?" Sam asked, leaning over.

"Do you hear it? Ba-boom…ba-boom… It sounds like a heart beating. I think they buried poor George alive in here!"

Sam bounced up and pushed Derek into the grass. "Will you stop it!" He didn't know how he always fell for Derek's lame jokes.

"Gotcha, Sam!" Derek shouted.

"Shh! Be quiet, we don't want anyone coming over here and asking what we're doing. This place is a federal park or something. We could get arrested for messing with the grave of a signer of the Declaration of Independence."

"Actually, the sign out front said this is a National Historic Landmark. I notice these things," Derek said, proudly.

"Boys! Derek! Sam!" The brothers jumped as they heard their dad's voice ring out across the graveyard.

Derek wiped his hands on his pants and hopped to his feet. "We're coming! Come on, Sam! Move it!"

* * *

THE BOYS SLID into the wooden pew beside their parents toward the back of the church. Mom wasn't happy they were late. After all, it had been their idea to come there in the first place. She pulled the hat off Sam's head and frowned at Derek's dirty pants.

Derek nudged Sam in the side and pointed toward the front of the church. Several actors were standing in the aisles, arguing back and forth in English accents, using very formal-sounding words. They all wore the colonial clothes like the tour guide from their class trip.

"Do you see him?" Derek whispered.

Sam scanned back and forth, trying to pick out a familiar face. It was hard to tell since they were near the back, but he didn't recognize anyone.

A voice in the front of the church announced, "The floor recognizes the good gentleman from Hanover County, Mr. Henry."

"Mr. President, I move to propose an amendment!" shouted a loud voice from the left side of the room. The speaker rose from his bench and turned to address the crowd.

Sam gasped when he immediately recognized the man's face. He slouched down in his seat and lowered his head. He wished he still had his hat on.

"Look Sam, it's Patrick Henry!" pointed Derek in excitement. He turned and saw Sam slumped down in the bench. "What's the matter?"

"It's him!" Sam hissed. "That's the guy!"

"Wait, Patrick Henry is the guy who tried to grab you?" Derek whispered in astonishment. "I mean, not the real Patrick Henry, but the reenactment guy Patrick Henry?"

Sam nodded his head quickly.

"Whoa," muttered Derek. "That's not good."

Mom looked over, noticing Sam's pale face. "Honey, are you okay?" she whispered.

Sam shook his head and held his stomach with his hand. This was a huge mistake. What was he thinking coming back here so soon?

"I think he's feeling sick," said Derek.

"Okay, go out with him to the bathroom, but don't wander off," whispered Dad with a sigh. "Please try to be quiet so you don't disrupt the program any more than you already have."

Derek nudged Sam toward the aisle, and they crept toward the exit. Sam tried to open the heavy wooden door without anyone noticing, but it let out a loud groan that echoed through the room. He wanted to keep going, but he couldn't help looking back at the actors at the front of the room.

Jerry was waving his arms in his Patrick Henry role, shouting about how the colony couldn't protect itself from England. When the noise from the door rang out, though, he raised his head. His eyes locked with Sam's. A streak of fear shot through Sam's body, and he froze in his tracks.

"Death!" yelled Jerry. "Death is waiting at our doors if we do not build up our own rations and militia!"

"Come on, Sam, go!" Derek pushed them through the doorway into the sunlight.

Sam ran over to a tree and bent over with his hands on his knees. He couldn't stop breathing fast. Maybe he was hyperventilating.

Derek patted Sam on the back. "This is perfect! Are you ready?"

"What? Are you crazy?" Sam looked up. "We have to get out of here. Did you hear what he yelled when we left? 'Death is at the door!' He was looking right at me, Derek!"

"Relax, Sam, that was just part of the show. He wasn't really looking at you. It *is* perfect, don't you see?" Derek pulled the program out of his pocket. "Bad Patrick Henry is busy in there with the reenactment. The show is supposed to last for an hour, and they're not even halfway through it. That means we've got at least thirty minutes to explore and look for clues without having to worry about him."

"Unless," Sam moaned, "he comes out in the middle of the program and looks for us. Then *he* has thirty minutes to kill us with no one else around!"

Sam pictured Jerry digging up a fresh grave just for him.

"He can't do that," said Derek. "He's Patrick Henry, the star of the show. And look!" He turned the paper program around in his hands, showing the page to Sam. "We know his name. Right here, see. Patrick Henry is played by Jerry Millburn."

"Great," Sam said. "Well, let's get out of here before Patrick, Jerry, or whoever he is comes after us."

Derek checked his watch. "We still have time. Come on, we need to go down to the basement where they were digging. I'll bet there's something really cool in that spot. Maybe it's a Babe Ruth rookie card. That would be worth a fortune!"

"Wrong century, Derek, but I agree that it must be something pretty special. Otherwise Jerry and his henchmen wouldn't have been in there digging."

Sam reluctantly followed Derek. He looked warily over his shoulder, half expecting Patrick Henry to jump out with a musket and shoot his head off. Sam tried to picture him inside the church talking away about liberty and death. He looked up and caught a glimpse of his brother walking around the corner toward the back of the church.

"Derek, wait!" he hollered, running to catch up.

Derek stood next to an old door at the back of the

building. "Is this the door you went through when you saw them?" he asked.

"Yeah, but there's a padlock on it."

Derek grinned wide. "You mean this one?" He opened his hand and held out the lock. "It was unlocked already. Come on!"

Derek pulled open the door. The same dim light hung over the stone floor. Sam got the chills when he saw the spot where Jerry had grabbed him. They scampered down the hallway to where the men had been working. The big empty space was still in the rock.

"So let's assume there wasn't anything in the wall where they looked," said Derek. "If something was supposed to be under where Patrick Henry spoke, where else could it be?"

A loud bang came from the floor above them. The boys heard loud voices shouting from the reenactment. A cloud of dirt and dust rained onto their heads, and Derek started coughing. Sam looked up and scanned the ceiling. It was lower than a modern building, with wide wooden beams stretching from one side of the small room to the other. From down there, it was impossible to tell where Patrick Henry would have been standing.

Derek looked back up at the ceiling. "Maybe it's not in the wall. Maybe it's in the floor."

"I think they'd have seen it if it was on the floor, Derek. And we can't go up there! That's where *he* is."

"No, not *on* the floor, *in* the floor – like under a floorboard or something." He moved over to the wall and looked up. "Come over here. See if I can lift you up to reach the floorboards."

"What? No way! You do it! We need to get out of here. The reenactment is going to end soon."

"Come on, trust me. I have a plan," Derek said. Sam hated it when Derek had a plan. They often worked, but they were usually painful in the process.

He begrudgingly came over to where Derek was standing and lifted his foot up onto his brother's clasped hands. Sam heaved himself up against the wall until his head was nearly touching the ceiling.

"Okay," Sam whispered, "I'm up here. Now what?" He kept his voice low since he was just underneath the floor of the church. His left foot was resting on Derek's shoulder while his right was propped against the stone wall. His head brushed against the coarse wood streaked with cobwebs and dirt.

"See if you can feel anything up there along the boards," Derek said.

Sam looked around but couldn't see much of anything in the shadows. He stretched his arm out into the empty space between the floor joists, feeling around with his hand. He tried one direction and then another, but all he felt were cobwebs and rough edges of wood.

Finally, he leaned all the way toward the basement

wall's edge. He positioned himself between the stone and the wood beams, right above where the men had been digging. Beneath him, Derek unexpectedly shifted his weight and Sam lost his balance. He frantically reached out and clung to the beam for dear life. Under his hand, against the beam, he felt something different – something soft.

"I think I've got something!"

The sound of clapping rang out above them.

"Great! Grab it and get down!" said Derek.

Sam gave the object a light tug, pulling it loose from its place against the wood. He drew his arm out and jumped down from the ledge.

In his hand was some kind of old scroll or tube of paper, like when he rolled up a poster in his room. The paper was yellowed and crinkly. It must have been up there for a long time.

"Is that parchment paper?" asked Derek.

"I don't know, but it seems pretty old," said Sam. "We can look at it later. Let's get out of here before somebody finds us."

Sam tucked the roll of paper into his jacket, and they hustled out into the daylight. The church bells were ringing and people were filing out the side door of the church. The boys scurried behind a gravestone and watched for their parents. Some of the performers were lined up along the back sidewalk, ready to shake hands and greet the audience.

Sam couldn't see Jerry yet, nor was there any sign of their parents. Maybe Jerry had them cornered! He could be questioning them this very minute!

The bells quieted, and finally Mom and Dad exited the building. Sam let out a sigh as he took a few steps toward them. Jerry emerged from the doorway right behind them.

Sam stopped in his tracks.

"I'll meet you by the car," Sam said to Derek, starting down the hill. Derek hustled over to Mom and Dad to hurry them along.

Sam walked quickly down the sidewalk, through the gate, and out to the street where they'd parked. He started to move around a man working on the brick wall below the fence. The man scooted backward just as Sam passed by, and they bumped arms.

"Sorry," said Sam, continuing on. He turned his head to look back at the man. It was one of the men who had been digging in the basement! Startled, Sam tripped on a crack and tumbled down onto the sidewalk.

The man looked up, and Sam knew he'd been recognized. "Hey, kid, I know you!"

Sam had to get out of there. He jumped to his feet and started running. He reached their minivan, but it was locked! He turned back, expecting for the man to grab him at any second. To his surprise, though, the man was going in the opposite direction. In fact, he was running up the steps toward the church. Where was he going?

Sam turned and saw Derek hustling Mom and Dad toward the van. They must have come around the other side of the block. Sam waved his arms wildly. "Come on! We have to go!"

"What is the big hurry?" Mom asked. "First you beg to come here, then you miss nearly the entire program. Now you want to race off like our house is on fire?"

"You boys missed a good program," said Dad. "You could have learned a lot in there."

"Oh, don't worry, we learned a lot," Derek assured them as he climbed into his seat.

"Shut the door, Derek! Come on, let's go!" Sam shouted. He looked up at the church. The man from the sidewalk was pointing at their van with Jerry beside him. As both men started running toward the street, Sam ducked below the window out of sight.

"Step on it, Dad!"

The men raced down the steps as the van pulled away from the curb. They ran out into the road, but they were too late.

Derek leaned out the window. "I know your phone number, Jerry!" he screamed, shaking his fist back at the two men.

"What in the world?" called out Mom from the front seat. "Derek, get back in the car!"

Derek sank back into his seat with a smile.

Mom turned around in her seat and looked at the road behind them. "Who are you yelling at? Is that one of the actors from the program?"

"Boys, sit back and buckle your seatbelts right now!" Dad ordered. "Derek, no more outbursts. That's no way to speak to anyone."

Sam turned and frowned at Derek. "Did you just say you know his phone number?"

Derek just smiled.

"Do you?"

"No, I don't know why I said that!" Derek said, chuckling. "I wanted to scare him and that's just what came out."

Sam started laughing so hard he ended up coughing. "Oh, I'm sure you scared him with that! Next time you can tell him you're going to send him an email!"

Sam exhaled loudly. It felt good to laugh again. He reached inside his jacket, relieved to find the rolled-up paper still safely tucked away. He couldn't look at it with Mom and Dad in the car, so he sat back and closed his eyes. It could wait until they got home.

THE LETTER

I t was already dinnertime by the time they arrived home. Sam ran up to his room and placed the rolled-up paper under his bed. He hustled back downstairs, trying to look casual. He didn't want Mom and Dad to get suspicious and make him confess to having a document from the American Revolution hidden in his room. They may not understand.

As the family ate dinner, Dad described the rest of the program that they missed. "Patrick Henry was really the founder with the passion that inspired the other members of the Virginia Convention to join the war effort. It was pretty exciting to be sitting right there in the same room where it actually took place and have him talk about joining the revolution."

"Why would anyone not want to join the revolution?" asked Derek. "Didn't they want America to be its own country?"

"Well, it wasn't quite that simple," explained Mom. "A lot of people didn't like the fact that we'd be at war with England. Remember, America was originally an English colony. Many of the colonists had recently come from England and still considered it to be their homeland.

"Some were scared that if the colonies declared war on England, they would be crushed. Many thought there weren't enough guns, bullets, or trained men to fight. The British had the greatest military might in the world at that time. The colonies were really just made up of a scattered collection of farmers and common folk who didn't know how to fight a war."

"But we had George Washington! Wasn't he the general?" asked Derek.

"Yes, he did lead the American troops," Mom replied. "He was also from Virginia and was played by one of the actors. He stood up and said he would support joining the revolution, offering to be their military leader."

"Was Thomas Jefferson there too? Didn't he write the Declaration of Independence?" asked Sam.

"That's right," said Dad. "A lot of the great Founding Fathers were from right here in Virginia."

"How about George Wythe?" asked Derek. "We saw

his grave out in the cemetery. It said he was one of the signers of the Declaration."

"I don't know a lot about him," answered Mom, "but I think you're right that he was a signer. There's a house in Colonial Williamsburg named after him, and I think he was a professor at William and Mary."

"William and Mary who?" asked Sam.

"That's where she went to college, dummy," yelled Derek. "Duh, Sam!"

"Hey, don't call me a dummy. You didn't even know how to pronounce George Wythe!"

"Okay, okay," said Dad. "Stop arguing. I think you knew that Mom went to the College of William and Mary, Sam. You probably just forgot. It's the oldest college in the country."

"The second oldest," corrected Mom. "Harvard's the oldest."

"It's the second oldest college in the country," restated Dad. "So several of the Virginia founders were associated with it."

"Yeah, the gravestone said that Wythe taught Thomas Jefferson and a few other guys," said Sam. "That's pretty cool. We should go visit Williamsburg again sometime. Mom, you're always wanting to go back and see your old college. What was that place you lived in called – your fraternity house?"

Dad choked on his drink of water and Mom laughed. "It was a sorority house, Sam. Boys live in a fraternity house."

"I don't know if we'll be taking any more family history trips for a while after the attention that you two paid to the reenactment today," said Dad, wiping his mouth. "Your mom and I enjoyed it, but you hardly saw any of it."

"I'm sorry, Dad, that was my fault," said Sam. "I was really feeling sick all of a sudden. I think it was those benches with the high walls all around. They were making me feel catastrophic."

Derek smacked his forehead and laughed, "You mean claustrophobic!"

"Yeah, that too."

"We'll think about it," said Mom. "It *would* be fun to get back on campus. We could stop and see your Great-Aunt Karen too. She lives right there in town next to the colonial section. She's been asking to see us since we moved to Virginia."

Sam wasn't sure how fun that would be. He had only met old Aunt Karen a few times, but as far as he could remember, *fun* was not a word he would use to describe her. She lived in one of those old houses where everything was an antique. Everybody had to walk around carefully so they didn't break something important. He wondered if her house might actually be part of Colonial Williamsburg. The last time they were there, he and Derek had just played outside while Mom and Dad talked to her.

"And," continued Mom, "we could show you where your dad and I were married. You were too young to remember the last time we went by the Wren Chapel. It's where everything started for our family." She looked off into the distance as if she were remembering some grand event like winning the World Series or the Super Bowl.

"As long as there's no kissing. Please, no kissing," Sam said.

"We'll try to keep the romance under control, Sam. Don't worry," Dad laughed.

"And we can see George Wythe's house while we're there, too, right?" asked Derek. "I really want to see it since we saw his grave today."

"Really? You think that would be interesting?" asked Dad, raising his eyebrow in surprise. "I thought you'd be too busy having long talks with Aunt Karen about her antique collection."

"Dad!" the boys yelled in unison.

"Actually," continued Dad, "I thought you might be more interested in stopping by, oh, I don't know, maybe the waterpark on the way home?"

"Waterpark! Yeah, that would be awesome! Sweet! We should definitely do that, too," shouted Sam. "Can we really?"

"Let us talk about it," said Mom.

Sam could already tell that she was going to say yes. She still had that faraway look in her eyes that said she really wanted to get back to her old college.

* * *

AFTER DINNER, Sam and Derek ran up to their room and shut the door. Derek brought his desk lamp over to the middle of the rug, and they pulled the old paper out from under the bed. As Sam carefully unrolled it, Derek gently rested some of their small baseball trophies on each corner to hold it down.

In addition to the letter, there was another object rolled up inside the paper. It was shaped like a rectangle, about the size of a ruler. It felt thin like a piece of cardboard, but it wasn't cardboard. Sam decided it must be some slender type of wood, like the kind for model airplanes. The wood framed a clear center section with a strange series of holes and tiny lines.

"What is *that* thing?" asked Sam. "The middle looks like plastic."

"It can't be plastic. I don't think that was even invented back then!" said Derek.

They turned and stared at the paper. It was old and thin. Words were written across it with a slanted-looking cursive like what Sam had been practicing in Mrs. H's class. It was hard to read, and Sam worried that it would tear if they touched it too much. Derek began to read the letter aloud.

June 25, 1806

Dear Sir,

It pains me greatly to learn only too late that you have left this life, my teacher and friend. My only encouragement is the earnest belief that you are presently in a place much greater than this. I shall do everything in my power to track down the truth about that ne'er-do-well, Mr. Sweeney, who has disgraced the Wythe family name. Even in this time of sorrow, it does my heart well to remember the courageous fight for liberty we all have undertaken and has since become manifest. I give back to you now, even in death, this key to the marvelous device that you demonstrated in your study. You'll remember that it leads to the early version of our great declaration, the one I sent with you upon your return to Williamsburg before the great signing. I trust that it shall rest safely in its own shallow grave to commemorate our greatest achievement. May you find peace with the Almighty.

Your friend and servant,

Thomas Jefferson

After Derek finished reading the letter, the boys were

silent. Sam didn't understand some of the fancy words, but he followed the general idea. It was a letter from Thomas Jefferson to George Wythe. Jefferson must have written it after Wythe's death, but it was still over 200 years old.

"Wow," Derek exclaimed, breaking the silence. "A real letter from Thomas Jefferson! That is heavy stuff!"

Sam held up the rectangular object. Their lamp light flowed through the tiny holes, making lots of sparkles against the wall. They looked like the stars on the ceiling of a planetarium.

"Does this seem like a key to you?" Sam asked.

"Not like any key I've ever seen," said Derek. "It must somehow work together with a device in Wythe's study."

Sam looked back at the letter. "It talked about that Sweeney guy again, just like the men in the basement. What did it call him?" He looked back at the letter. "A 'ne'er-do-well.' What's that?"

"Beats me! But whatever a 'ne-er' is, Sweeney's not doing it well." Derek laughed at his own joke. He did that a lot. He walked over to the bookshelf and pulled out the big dictionary. He flipped to the 'N' section and ran his finger down the page.

"Let's see... *Ne'cessitously, ne'er*, here we go, *ne'er-do-well* – *an idle, worthless person; good-for-nothing.*" He looked up from the book. "Sam, you ne'er-do-well!"

"Ha ha," muttered Sam. "Wow, I guess that Sweeney

guy is a real creep. At least Thomas Jefferson thought so. We need to find out who he is. But if we ask Dad to use his computer, he's going to ask us why."

"You should call your girlfriend," Derek suggested with a smile.

"Who?" asked Sam, his face flushing. Whenever he got embarrassed, his face turned as red as a tomato.

"You know, that girl in your class who was on your field trip. You said she knew all about history. Maybe she can help us with this."

"Caitlin?" said Sam in disbelief. "I can't call Caitlin on the phone! And she's NOT my girlfriend! I don't even like her. She was just in my group on the trip. She is *totally* annoying."

"Well, we have to do something. We're sitting here in our room with Thomas Jefferson's letter. This is an emergency!"

Sam thought about Derek's idea. "She did say she wanted to do some research," he admitted.

"Perfect!" shouted Derek. "What's her phone number?"

"Why don't you ask Jerry? You seem to know his number."

"Very funny, Sam. Seriously, what's her number? You need to call her."

"I don't have her number memorized, Derek. Let me go find the school directory." Sam coolly walked downstairs and scanned the bookshelf next to the microwave. He pulled out the thin red directory with one hand and grabbed the phone with the other. Then he hustled out of the kitchen and back upstairs before his parents could get suspicious.

THE PHONE CALL

After Sam found Caitlin's name under '*M*' for Murphy, he picked up the phone and paused. He'd never called a girl before. Not that it was a big deal, but it just seemed a little weird. He certainly had never thought about calling Caitlin of all people. She normally drove him crazy, and not in a good way. Having Derek stare at him across the bedroom with a big goofy grin definitely wasn't helping either.

Finally, he dialed the number. After a of couple rings, a woman's voice answered.

"Hi, this is Caitlin's home? I mean, this is Sam. Is Caitlin home?"

"Sam," the woman's voice repeated, "Sam who?"

"Sam Jackson," he said, getting red all over again. "Um, I'm in Caitlin's class. I have a homework question." He knew that wasn't entirely true, but it *was* related to research and history. Those were school kinds of things even if it wasn't exactly homework. Plus it all started on a school field trip.

"Oh, Sam Jackson!" exclaimed the woman, whom he assumed was Caitlin's mother, like she was telling other people in the room who was calling.

Sam felt sick.

"Yes, I heard that you were on the field trip with Caitlin this week," she said. "Did you have a good time? Caitlin has been talking all about it. I'm so glad that you two have become such good friends."

"Yes, ma'am."

A man of few words – that was Sam. Good friends? What the heck had Caitlin had been saying about the trip? He'd certainly never thought of her as his friend or anything like that. He wondered if she'd told her parents about what happened to him in the basement.

Derek threw a pillow at him from across the room and motioned with his hands to get on with it already.

"Okay, Sam. Here's Caitlin. Goodbye." She sounded much too happy for his liking.

A softer voice came on the line.

"Hel-lo?"

It was Caitlin. The way she said hello made it sound like she couldn't understand in a million years why he would be calling her. Sam almost hung up. This was just another of Derek's stupid ideas.

He cleared his throat and nearly sneezed. "Uh, hi, Caitlin. It's Sam."

"Yes, I know, Sam. Why are you calling my *house*?" She emphasized 'house,' like he should have expressly known never to call her at her house of all places.

Sam put his hand over the phone and whispered to Derek. "She doesn't want to talk to me. This was a bad idea!"

"Here, let me talk to her," said Derek, striding across the room.

Before Sam could stop him, Derek snatched the phone right out of his hand. Sam tried to grab it back, but Derek pushed him away and walked back to the other side of the room.

"Hi, Caitlin, this is Sam's older brother, Derek. How are you on this fine evening?"

Sam smacked his hand against his forehead. This was going to be a disaster. He couldn't hear what Caitlin was saying any more. Derek's side was bad enough.

"Sam tells me that you were involved in the incident that he had at P. Henry's church the other day..."

P. Henry? Who did Derek think he was, a historical rapper? Derek was trying so hard to act cool. Sam was sure that she'd hang up on him.

"Anyway," Derek continued, "Sam says that you're great with research. We're in a bit of a jam with our computer access right now. Do you think you could help us out?"

There was silence while Derek waited for a response. "You will? Perfect! Thanks a lot. Here, let me put you on speaker so that Sam can hear you, too."

Derek pushed a button on the phone and handed it back to Sam. With a wink, he made a motion with his finger like a gun that meant everything was cool.

"Hello?" So now she was back to saying that again?

"Hi, Caitlin," Sam jumped in. "So anyway, we found a letter when we went back to the church. It seems to have been written by Thomas Jefferson to George..."

"Thomas Jefferson!" she screamed. "Are you serious?"

Man, she was excited. She sure didn't sound like the typical snobby Caitlin from class.

"Uh, Caitlin," interrupted Derek. "We have to ask that you keep this information top secret. You can't tell *anybody* right now, not even your parents."

"Why not?" she asked suspiciously. "You didn't steal something, did you? Was Billy part of this? Is he there with you right now?"

"No, Billy isn't here," Sam assured her. "And we didn't really steal anything either, we just found this letter."

He gave her a quick run-down of how they'd found the letter at the church. Then he read it to her. She corrected him on a few of the longer words just like he figured she would. He was happy to at least know what *ne'er-do-well* meant in case she asked him.

"That's unbelievable!" Caitlin said, after Sam finished reading. "You have to tell someone, maybe the museum."

"We're trying to figure this out on our own first," said Derek. "We've actually done this kind of thing before. You may have seen us in the newspaper last year. We were the ones who recovered the lost coin collection for the museum."

"Oh, that's right," said Caitlin. "I do remember seeing that."

Sam rolled his eyes.

"So, Caitlin," Sam said, trying to get back on track. "Can you look up this Sweeney guy on your computer and tell us what it says?"

"Sure, I can do that. I have a laptop in my room. Don't you?"

"Uh, no, we don't." Sam muttered. Mom and Dad had a policy about no TV or computer in the boys' bedroom. It didn't seem fair since everybody, even Caitlin, apparently, had one. Mom and Dad said something about keeping track of what they're looking at and encouraging 'family time,' but Sam didn't quite get it.

"Okay, let me look here," said Caitlin, already typing away on her computer. "Do you know his full name other than just Sweeney?"

"No," said Derek. "That's all the letter says. Mr. Sweeney."

"It did say something about sharing George Wythe's name, though," added Sam. "Maybe you could search for Sweeney and George Wythe."

"Okay, let me see." Sam heard Caitlin hitting buttons on her computer. Then there was a short pause as she read to herself.

"Oh my gosh!" she exclaimed.

"What?" both the boys yelled together.

"What is it?" Sam said again.

"You're not going to believe this," said Caitlin. "It says that in 1806, there was a George Sweeney on trial in Richmond. Sweeney, the grand-nephew of George Wythe, one of the Founding Fathers of the United States, was acquitted of murdering Wythe, who died of arsenic poisoning!"

"Whoa, I didn't know Wythe had a grand-nephew! I've never even heard of that before," said Derek.

Sam smacked him in the arm. "Stop it, Derek, be serious. Aren't you listening? Wythe was poisoned by his own family! No wonder Thomas Jefferson called Sweeney a worthless person."

"That's terrible to have such an important man killed like that," said Caitlin. "This article says that Sweeney was found not guilty. That's what acquitted means, Sam. The only witness to the poisoning was one of Wythe's slaves.

Back then, courts couldn't hear the testimony of black witnesses. That's terrible. Wythe told his friends on his death bed, 'I am murdered.'"

"That's creepy," said Derek. "This Wythe character has quite a story."

"So what are you going to do now?" Caitlin asked. "Have you thought about the rest of the letter?"

Sam had been so wrapped up in hearing about George Sweeney, he almost forgot to consider what else the letter said.

"Read me the middle part again," said Caitlin. "Where he was giving something back to Wythe."

Sam found the part she was talking about and began to read the letter aloud:

"*I give back to you now, even in death, this key to the marvelous device you demonstrated in your study. You'll remember it leads to the early version of our great declaration, the one I sent with you upon your return to Williamsburg before the great signing.*"

"Let me look up George Wythe and Williamsburg now," said Caitlin.

They heard a few moments of typing.

"He must be talking about the Wythe House in Williamsburg. It says that's where George Wythe lived."

"Hey, that's the place Mom and Dad talked about at dinner," said Derek. "Have you ever been there, Caitlin?"

"I think I've walked by it. I haven't been inside,

although they probably give tours," she answered. "You two have been to Williamsburg, haven't you? It's only like an hour away. They have all kinds of interesting…"

"Yeah, we've been there," Sam interrupted her. He'd heard Caitlin give speeches about "interesting" things before, and they didn't have that much time to talk tonight.

"We were there when we were younger," said Sam. "Our mom went to college in Williamsburg, and our parents got married at the chapel there."

"I don't think we cared much about this stuff the last time we were there, though," admitted Derek. "It seemed kind of boring. I do remember putting my head in that big wooden thing. That was cool!"

"The stocks," said Sam. He recalled Mom and Dad taking a picture of each of them with their head and arms stuck in the wooden constraints. "Maybe we should have left you there, Derek."

"Oh my gosh, I just thought some more about the letter," said Caitlin. "Do you know what he must have meant by the early version of the declaration?" Her voice was brimming with anticipation. She didn't wait for them to answer. "The Declaration of Independence!" she shrieked over the phone.

"Whoa," said Derek. "Is it the real Declaration of Independence? Maybe all this time, the country has been looking at the wrong document! Maybe we're not officially Americans. We could actually be part of Spain!"

"What I don't understand," said Caitlin, ignoring Derek like she often ignored Billy, "is why the letter says Jefferson sent something with Wythe to Williamsburg before the great signing. They signed the Declaration in Philadelphia. Why would he go back to Williamsburg before it was signed? I'll have to do more research and get back to you at school. This is too much – I have to go!"

"Okay, thanks..." Sam tried to say, but she had already hung up. Girls were weird.

There was a knock on their door.

"Boys, did you take the phone from the kitchen? I can't find it down here anywhere."

It was Mom!

"Quick – get that letter rolled up and under the bed!" Derek whispered.

"Uh, yeah, I think it's in here somewhere, hang on," Sam stalled.

"What are you boys doing in there?" Mom called through the door.

"We're looking up words in the dictionary," said Derek, in a half-truth. He watched Sam put the letter carefully under the bed without tearing it.

"Okay, come in!"

"Were you on the phone?" asked Mom.

"No, we were just stumping each other with words," Derek lied. "Sam is a ne'er-do-well."

"Really! Well, that's a pretty big word. You've been known to be a troublemaker yourself, sir," Mom said, laughing. "It's time to get ready for bed. It's late, and you both have school tomorrow."

"Okay," answered Derek.

"Here's your phone, Mom," said Sam.

After the lights were out, Sam looked over at Derek's bed. "What are we going to do?"

"We need to figure out the part about Wythe's study in Williamsburg. There's something hidden there, but I don't know what." Derek yawned loudly and turned over in his bed. "I've got to go to sleep. We can figure this out tomorrow after school. It's not going anywhere tonight."

Sam lay in his bed holding the "key" that didn't look like a key. He stared at the ceiling. How could he go to sleep with so much to think about? They had found something amazing here. It was even bigger than the rare coins they found last summer. He had a piece of history right in his hands. A letter and a clue from one of the most important people in the nation.

Sam agreed with Derek – they *had* to go to Williamsburg. He hoped Mom and Dad wouldn't change their minds. What could be in George Wythe's study? Could it really lead to the Declaration of Independence? That didn't seem possible. He'd read in his textbook at school that the Declaration of Independence was on display in Washington.

He imagined George Wythe, such an important guy, lying in bed, yelling about being poisoned by his good-for-nothing grand-nephew, Sweeney. Not the way that you want to go. And poor George wasn't even that famous. Well, at least Sam hadn't known about him before Caitlin pointed out his grave.

Certainly he wasn't as famous as his student, Thomas Jefferson. Jefferson went on to be one of the most famous people in the country. He even became President, for goodness sake. Sam and his family had visited the Jefferson Memorial in Washington. He didn't remember seeing a Wythe Memorial. It just goes to show that life isn't fair. Jefferson ended up on the nickel, and Wythe ended up poisoned.

Sam tried to think about the letter some more, but his head was starting to hurt. His eyes were heavy. Before long, despite his swirling thoughts, he was asleep.

THE DECLARATION

"Children, that's enough talking. In your seats right now!" yelled Mrs. Haperwink.

The pledge of allegiance was about to start, followed by the morning announcements over the loudspeaker.

Sam was tired again. He still wasn't sleeping, which was twice as bad for him as it would be for some people. Normally he slept like a rock. But when he didn't sleep well, he really felt terrible.

As the bell rang, Caitlin was trying to get his attention from across the aisle. She mouthed the words 'I need to talk to you.' Sam wrote 'recess' on the top of his notebook and held it up to her as he stood for the flag. There was no sign of Billy, but he was often late, so that was nothing new.

I pledge allegiance, to the flag, of the United States of America.

As if that were his introduction, Billy burst around the corner. Realizing that he was interrupting the pledge, he stopped in the doorway and came to attention with his hand over his heart. Mrs. H gave him a critical look.

And to the Republic, for which it stands, one nation, under God, indivisible, with liberty and justice for all.

As Billy sauntered over to his desk, Sam couldn't help but notice that word again in the pledge – "liberty."

It was following him.

He supposed it was better than having a word like "death" or "destruction" follow him, but it did remind him of Jerry. Sam had been dreaming about him all night. Bad Patrick Henry, as Derek had taken to calling Jerry.

Third grade recess was late in the day, and lunch was even later. It seemed really stupid to Sam. Derek's fourth grade class ate lunch at eleven, but they didn't have their recess until the last period of the day. It didn't make any sense. He wondered if Ms. Saltwater had engineered the schedule just so the day could be a bit more miserable for everyone. He wouldn't put it past her.

As soon as they reached the playground, Caitlin ran over and grabbed Sam's arm. "I have to talk to you!"

"Okay, okay. I want to talk to you too, but let go of my arm." Sam wriggled loose from her grasp before anyone noticed.

"Sam, come on, the game is going to start," yelled Brandon Perth from the soccer field. "Or maybe you're going to play in the girls' game today!"

Several of the guys laughed and pointed to him standing next to Caitlin.

"Jackson, come on," Billy said as he jogged by. He pointed to the soccer field. "You were supposed to be co-captain today for choosing teams."

"I don't think I'm going to play today," Sam answered.

"You're what?" yelled Billy. No one ever turned down the chance to be captains for soccer.

"Caitlin and I have some stuff to talk about from the church, remember?" Sam swore that Billy came to school with only half a brain sometimes.

"Church? But today's Monday," replied Billy, until a wave of recognition slowly came over his face. "Oh, that church! Right, hey, I'm coming too."

The other boys noticed Billy walking off with Sam and Caitlin.

"Aw, forget it," yelled Brandon in disgust. "Reed, you're co-captain today in place of Sam. Let's go."

Sam sat down on the picnic bench next to the blacktop and turned to Caitlin. "So what did you find out about the letter?"

"Well, I did some more searching about why George Wythe would go home to Williamsburg before the signing," started Caitlin.

"You found a letter! When did you do that?" asked Billy in surprise.

"I'll tell you later," replied Sam. He turned back to Caitlin. "Go on, what did you find out about Williamsburg?"

"So, as you know," she paused and sighed at Billy. "Well, as *some* of you know, the Founding Fathers were in Philadelphia at the Second Continental Congress on July 4, 1776, to sign the Declaration of Independence. It turns out that's not entirely true. They declared independence on July 4, but the actual document wasn't ready for the official signing until a few weeks later. They couldn't just hit *print* on their computer, you know."

"Could they take a picture on their phone?" asked Billy.

Caitlin sighed but continued. "Anyway, the document had to be engrossed, which I read means copying it onto parchment paper very neatly. It wasn't ready for the final signatures until August 2, 1776. That's almost a month later. By that time, George Wythe and several others had already returned home."

"I guess he had other things to do besides sit around Philadelphia waiting for the ink to dry," said Sam.

"Right, so he went back home to Williamsburg."

"To the George Wythe House," said Sam.

"Right. And you know what is *so* cool? Since Wythe wasn't there to sign the final document with everyone else, all the other members of the Virginia delegation left a space before their signatures so that Wythe could sign on top. They were showing him respect."

"Wow, that is cool," said Sam. "So then according to the letter, Thomas Jefferson gave Wythe some kind of early version of the Declaration of Independence, and then hid it in his house in Williamsburg?"

This was exciting, thought Sam. Complicated, but exciting.

"That would be my guess," replied Caitlin. "Tell me more about the key you found with the letter. Is it some kind of map?"

"A treasure map?" asked Billy.

"No, it wasn't like that," Sam answered. "It's some kind of tool the shape of a ruler. And it has these strange markings on it that sparkle when the light shines through it. Derek and I can't figure it out. The letter said it was something that went with a device in Wythe's study."

"I wonder what that could be?" Caitlin said.

"I have no idea," Sam said. "I hope we can figure it

out if we go to Williamsburg. Derek and I are still trying to get our parents to take us there this weekend."

"What about the guys who were chasing you?" asked Billy. "Aren't they're looking for the same thing?"

Sam wished that Billy hadn't brought Jerry up. His stomach did a somersault again. Surely Jerry couldn't know that Sam had the Jefferson letter. But he could still be trying to find it. Maybe he was trying to find Sam too! Sam tried not to think about it.

"I wonder how Jerry knows about all of this in the first place?" asked Caitlin.

"I don't know, and right now, I don't really care," said Sam. "We have Jefferson's letter, and he doesn't. We're one step ahead of him, and I'd like to keep it that way."

NINE

THE DRIVE

S am and Derek managed to convince their parents to take a trip to Colonial Williamsburg that weekend. It hadn't been too hard. During the week, they saw Mom pulling out old photos and going through boxes of clothes she used to wear in college. They heard Dad whistle as she tried on some jean shorts that had been cut up with scissors on the bottom.

It was going to be their fifteen-year wedding anniversary in the fall, so they were definitely getting all romantic. It was fine with Sam, even if it did include some gross kissing. The more they were caught up in their mushy memories, the less likely they would be to notice Derek and him snooping around for clues at the Wythe House.

Williamsburg was only an hour or so away, but Dad wanted to get an early start because of traffic. He said they weren't the only family who wanted to see people run around in colonial costumes and check out old buildings.

That was probably true, thought Sam, but they were the only ones there to discover a secret historical document at the Wythe House.

Once they were motoring down the highway, Dad glanced up at them in the rearview mirror. "Let's play the license plate game," he suggested.

The boys groaned that they'd rather watch a movie.

"Nope, no movies on this trip," replied Dad. "We're stepping back into history. Did you know when Mom and I were kids there were no DVD players in cars? We read books, played games, and even talked to each other. Can you imagine that? It was crazy!"

Sam rolled his eyes. He'd heard this speech many times before. Next Dad was going to say he walked five miles to school, barefoot, in the snow. Plus it was uphill both ways.

"Come on, this is the perfect road to play the license plate game on," Dad said, undaunted by their lack of enthusiasm. "Williamsburg is a huge tourist area, which means people drive from all over the country to go there on vacation. Let's see how many different states we can find. Sam, what's your prediction?"

"Seventy-two," said Sam without even thinking about it.

Derek laughed and poked Sam in the ribs. "States,

Sam. There aren't even seventy-two states all together. The most you could find is fifty."

"Oh, right," said Sam, feeling a bit stupid even though he hadn't been trying. He thought about the question a little harder. "Well, I don't think it's very likely we'd find a car from Hawaii, since that's all the way across the ocean."

"But it's still possible," argued Derek. "Someone could be from Hawaii."

"They could *be* from Hawaii," said Sam, "but they wouldn't have their car here. You can't drive across the ocean to Virginia."

"But it's *possible*," Derek repeated.

Sam hated when they got into arguments like this. Derek always had to win no matter what.

"Nope. It's not." Sam dug in.

"Dad, tell Sam that it *is* possible for a car from Hawaii to be on this road."

"Well, I suppose it's possible," said Dad, "but not overly likely. Technically, if someone really wanted to spend time on the mainland, they could have their car brought over on a ship. But it would be expensive."

"See, Sam! It's possible!"

"Technically," Sam sniped back.

"*Technically* is still a yes," said Derek.

"Whatever."

"All right, let's look for those states, boys!" said Dad. "Look, there's Alabama. That's one."

"There's Virginia!" said Sam, sarcastically.

"Of course there's Virginia, we're *in* Virginia!" shouted Derek. He made an 'L' with his hand and held it up over his forehead. He mouthed the word 'lo-ser' at Sam and smirked.

Sam punched him in the stomach. Derek groaned and doubled over in his seat.

"Samuel! Why did you hit your brother?" Mom yelled from the front seat, twisting around to see the boys. "There's no need for that. Sit quietly if you don't want to play Dad's game."

It felt good to punch Derek, but Sam knew he shouldn't have. His brother was so obnoxious sometimes! Sam had been on edge all week with the craziness around the letter. Maybe he needed a vacation, but not one to Williamsburg.

Sam leaned his head against the window and watched the cars speed by. Somehow everything reminded him of their mystery, even the license plates.

A pickup truck from Pennsylvania went by with the words 'State of Independence' written along the bottom of its tag. A BMW from New York motored by with a picture of the Statue of Liberty in the middle of its plate.

Sam was about to close his eyes, when a bright yellow convertible caught his attention. Behind the wheel was a hippie-looking guy with long gray hair. A bunch of stickers were on his bumper. Sam stared closer to see the license plate. It definitely looked unusual. Was that a rainbow?

Derek saw it at the same time Sam did.

"Hawaii! Look, Sam, it's Hawaii! Ha! Ha! I told you!"

Unbelievable, thought Sam, as he closed his eyes.

TEN

THE WYTHE HOUSE

S am heard the engine turn off and the van doors
open. He raised his head and looked out the
window. His neck hurt. He must have drifted off to sleep
in an awkward position. They were in a parking lot
surrounded by cars and people were walking along the
road.

"Come on, Sam, we're here!" shouted Derek.

Sam climbed out of the van and joined his family on
the sidewalk. After Mom and Dad bought tickets, they
began walking along what seemed like the main street of
Colonial Williamsburg.

"This is Duke of Gloucester Street, boys," explained
Mom.

Sam looked up and down the wide road, sensing he
was back in another time. There were two horses tied to a
post and a carriage probably for giving rides to tourists. A

brown wooden barrel stood on each corner of the intersection instead of a modern-looking trashcan.

They'd arrived early, so there weren't many visitors yet. Those who were there were dressed in old-time colonial clothes. A woman with a wide skirt and white bonnet on her head set up a table of hand-woven baskets on one side of the street. A younger man with a tri-cornered hat tapped merrily on a drum as he marched along.

"Where should we go first?" asked Dad. "There's the Capitol, the Governor's Palace…oh, and you boys were asking about the George Wythe House, too. That's right over here before the Palace." He pointed to a square on the map.

Sam and Derek looked at each other quickly and nodded. "The Wythe House!" The boys were excited to look around and find clues in the study.

Mom and Dad laughed. "Okay, the Wythe House it is. I hope it's as great as you think it will be. I've actually never been inside," said Mom.

They walked around the corner, past a church, to a square brick house with a set of steps leading up to the front door.

Sam looked at a sign in the grass next to the sidewalk. "This is it! How do we get in?" He looked around for an entrance sign.

"Young man, are you looking to visit Mr. Wythe?"

called a voice from their left.

Sam jumped up in surprise. He turned and saw a man in a vest and long white socks. He was sitting on a bench in front of a small building next door.

Sam walked over to him. "Yes, we'd like to tour the Wythe House."

"Well, Mr. Wythe is presently away in Philadelphia, but I'm sure we can arrange for you to walk through his home."

Sam looked over at Mom and Dad, confused. They chuckled and gestured to keep talking to the man.

"He's away? Uh…isn't he dead?" Sam asked.

"Dead!" the old man shouted, jumping up from his bench. The small round glasses that rested on his nose nearly fell to the ground. "Where have you heard this news? Mr. Wythe has been serving in the Congress in Philadelphia! I've been told no such thing." He looked quite alarmed.

"I thought he was poisoned?" added Sam. Maybe this guy was older than he looked.

"Poisoned? Goodness, I hope not," the man continued. "Surely it wasn't from any food we prepared here. I just had some fresh strawberries this morning."

Sam was sure this guy had lost his marbles.

"Why don't you ask him today's date?" suggested Dad, smiling. "I think that might help with your confusion."

Derek turned back to the man. "What day is it?" he asked.

"Why, August 15, 1776, of course. Didn't you know? There's been quite a bit of excitement lately, what with everything happening up in Philadelphia. They say we declared our independence from the throne."

"Oh…" said Sam. Now it was all making more sense. The man must be playing a character on a particular date in history. That was cool. Confusing, but cool.

"Then why isn't Mr. Wythe here?" asked Sam. "I thought he came back to Williamsburg while they made the final copy of the declaration?"

The man paused for a moment, clearly surprised by Sam's historical knowledge. He quickly recovered with a smile. "Well, aren't you an informed young man!"

Sam grinned, feeling proud that he had impressed the man.

"I haven't met many children your age who know about Mr. Wythe," he commented.

"Oh sure," said Derek. "We know all about him. We saw his grave up at St. John's Church in Richmond."

"His grave!" the man shrieked.

Oh brother, here we go again, thought Sam.

"Never mind," laughed Derek. "What we'd really like to see is Mr. Wythe's study. We heard he had, I mean has, some very cool stuff up there."

"I'm not sure if it is cold in his study, if that's what

you mean by cool. But he certainly does have some interesting items," replied the man. "Mr. Wythe is a great admirer of Enlightenment philosophy. While primarily a teacher of the law, Mr. Wythe believes one should use all of the body's senses to be fully educated."

The man moved toward the white picket fence next to him. "But you said you wanted to see Mr. Wythe's study, didn't you? Let's proceed into the house, and I can show you."

The boys followed the man through the front door with Mom and Dad behind them. Sam looked around at the colorful rooms. The walls he could see were covered by wallpaper with fancy patterns. Bright greens, reds and blues. The floors were wide wooden boards with only a few small rugs under some of the tables. In the room to his left, a woman sat in a fancy parlor playing a dancing tune on the violin that sounded like Yankee Doodle.

They walked down the hall, peeking into the other rooms. The ceilings were especially high, and the windows were tall and set deep into the wall. It looked like seats were built into the bottom part of the windowsills. Each room had its own fireplace.

Sam pictured George Wythe and Thomas Jefferson sitting in front of the crackling logs discussing the revolution. Everything must have seemed so new and exciting back then.

The guide led them up a large wooden staircase to a

corner room. Sam could tell that this was Wythe's study. There was a table in the middle of the room filled with papers, drawings, and what looked like scientific equipment. A small jar had a feather sticking out of it. A map on a wall above the fireplace was labeled *Virginia and Maryland,* although it looked a lot different than the maps Sam had seen in his book at school. The boys wandered around the room and studied all of the items, trying to find something that fit the description given in Jefferson's letter.

"What's this thing?" Sam asked, pointing to a gold-colored metal instrument on the table. It looked similar to a small telescope, but it was mounted to a square piece of wood and pointing down toward the table. Some similar devices lay next to it.

"That," answered their tour guide, "is a microscope."

"It is?" said Derek. "It doesn't look like any microscope that I've ever seen."

"And why do you think that is?" asked the man.

"Because it's old," volunteered Sam. "It must be a very early kind of microscope."

"That's correct, young man. It is a form of what's

called a solar microscope." The guide pointed to a round piece of glass near the bottom. "You see this lens? It's the key to the microscope. It reflects the sun and illuminates whatever is on the slide under the main viewer. Remember, we must rely on the sun's power or a flame for our light."

Something that the man had said struck Sam. He had said it was the *key* to the microscope.

"That's pretty neat, isn't it, guys?" said Dad from the other side of the room. "Remember, they didn't have electricity back then."

"Since you boys are so astute in your learning, and since no one else is here at the moment, I'll show you one more interesting type of solar microscope that Mr. Wythe uses with his students." The guide picked up one of the other instruments from the table.

"This is a projecting solar microscope." He closed one of the window shutters, and Sam noticed for the first time that it had a round hole about the size of an orange cut out of the wood.

"What's that hole?" Derek asked. "Did someone hit the window with a baseball?"

The man looked up from the shutter. "What is this base-ball that you refer to? I'm not familiar with it."

Sam rolled his eyes. The date thing again. Baseball hadn't been invented back then. "So what is that hole?"

"Watch closely," answered the man. He took the

instrument from the table and fitted it on the shutter. The viewer part of the microscope fit directly in the hole, and there were clamps on both sides holding it in place.

"Is that so they can see outside when it's raining?" asked Derek.

The man laughed. "No, that's not it."

He picked up a rectangular piece of glass, about the shape of a small ruler, from the table and laid it in the contraption that was now mounted on the shutter.

"You place a glass slide into the viewer by the lens here. Then, when the sun comes through the window through the hole in the shutter, it goes into the lens of the microscope and projects the image from the slide up onto the wall. This allows others in the room to see an enlarged view of the tiny thing on the slide."

He maneuvered the shutter and turned a dial on the lens. "Like this!"

A round light appeared on the wall like a flashlight beam or a spotlight up on a stage. There was some kind of shadow in the middle that Sam couldn't quite make out.

"What is that?" Sam asked.

"That, gentlemen, is a flea. If the sun was a little brighter and we had all of the window shutters closed, you might be able to make it out more clearly. Amazing, isn't it? This is the latest innovation for the eighteenth century."

Sam looked at the light shining onto the wall. He thought about the key they had found and how it had made all the patterns of light on their bedroom wall through its tiny holes. What would happen, he wondered, if they put their key into the solar microscope just like their tour guide had showed them with the glass slide? It was roughly the same size. Even though it had just been a series of sparkles at home, maybe if it went through the lens, it would reveal something spectacular!

Sam was excited again. He caught Derek's attention, nodding toward the device. Derek's mouth opened in anticipation, and Sam could tell he understood Sam's message. But how could they get their key into the microscope without explaining it to everyone?

"Thank you for showing that to us," said Mom, motioning to the boys to say thank you. "That was a pretty special treat."

"Oh, yeah," said Derek. "Thank you."

"Thank you," said Sam.

"You're welcome, boys. Now let's head out and look at the gardens in the back of the house." The guide led them into the hallway with Mom and Dad following him out of the room.

Sam lingered a moment, fumbling with his bag. He pulled his key out and held it up to the microscope on the shutter. Although he didn't have time to place it in, he could tell it was the same size as the glass slide. He was pretty sure it would fit.

"Sam, come on!" Dad yelled from the hallway. Quickly Sam put the key back into his bag and hustled into the hall.

"Derek, wait up!" Sam called and ran down the stairs.

ELEVEN

THE GATHERING

Everyone followed the guide out the back door of the Wythe House. It opened up into a lush garden. Several brick walkways broke up strips of green grass behind the house.

"We'll be over here!" shouted the boys as they ran down the path toward a bench at the end of the garden. They sat underneath a covered trellis of ivy and vines for privacy.

Sam turned to Derek, nearly bursting with excitement. "Do you think the solar microscope was the device Thomas Jefferson was talking about in his letter?"

"It *has* to be. Did you see if the key fit the slide holder?"

"I held it up," answered Sam, "but there wasn't enough time to put it in. It seemed like it would fit, though."

"It must be a special kind of slide," said Derek. "Something Wythe developed just for the secret of the Declaration. We need to get back to that room. Maybe after it's closed we can sneak back in."

"I don't know if that's a good idea, Derek. We should tell someone first. This is a pretty important place. With all of the history here, they could call the FBI and charge us with damaging a national treasure!"

"But we might *find* them a national treasure!" said Derek. "That letter and whatever is on that slide are our insurance policy. We're not *stealing* anything, we're helping uncover something valuable *for* history. They'll be thanking us, trust me. But we'll never know if we don't get ourselves back in there."

Dad approached their meeting spot. "Come on, boys, let's finish looking around the gardens and then head over to the Governor's Palace."

Sam and Derek followed their parents through the gardens and a few small outbuildings. There was a kitchen, a stable, and a couple other separate structures. As they approached the Governor's Palace, the boys watched two men fill an old cannon with powder. They waited for a minute. Just when it seemed like nothing was going to happen, an enormous boom filled the air and shook the ground.

"Whoa," yelled Derek, covering his ears. "It's like fireworks on the Fourth of July!"

Inside the Palace was equally cool. The best part was the dark wood-paneled walls covered with rows and rows of old guns. There were hundreds of muskets and rifles, even shiny swords, all on display. It seemed like the colonists could have fought off the British using just the weapons on those walls.

After touring the Governor's house, Mom stopped to watch a demonstration on colonial basket weaving. Sam thought he'd rather sit and watch the grass grow. He was starting to like all of this history stuff, but basket weaving was where he drew the line.

He whispered to Dad that he was going to walk up the street for a few minutes, promising to meet them after the boring basket weaving session was over. Dad glanced up at the quiet wide streets and nodded his head. Sam turned, signaling for Derek to join him. The two wandered over to a marketplace stand and tried on some tri-cornered hats. Derek found a toy musket and pretended to shoot at Sam from behind a table stocked with homemade jams selling for fifteen dollars a jar.

A crowd was gathering outside the old church steps. Some of the colonial people were shouting. The boys put down the hats and muskets and walked over to see what was going on. Actors in costume were working their way through the crowd.

"Did you hear what they voted on over in Richmond

just last month?" chattered a woman. "It's only a matter of time now. I fear war will come quickly. That passionate speech by Mr. Patrick Henry has sparked a fight for liberty! Just like up in Boston."

Sam groaned at the sound of Patrick Henry's name. He hadn't thought about him for a while and wanted to keep it that way. George Wythe seemed much safer.

"Give me liberty or smell my breath?" said Derek, grinning at the woman. The lady just looked at him, confused. Derek seemed to like talking to these characters, but it still seemed a bit weird to Sam. He couldn't get used to the fact that they were supposed be from a different time period.

As they were listening to the woman, a colonial man in a green vest walked up behind the boys. He shouted into Sam's ear.

"The rumors say Mr. Henry will make a special visit to us today. He wants to talk more about the events up in Philadelphia at the Continental Congress. Some speak of even declaring independence from England!"

Patrick Henry would be here? Sam started to sweat.

Derek saw Sam's face whiten and leaned over. "Not *that* Patrick Henry, Sam. These are different actors."

Before Sam could answer, the door to the church opened and the crowd started buzzing. A man stepped out, waving his arms to the gathering. Sam craned his neck to see, but the lady in the dress was blocking his view.

"Citizens of Williamsburg, friends," cried the voice.

Sam froze. He knew that voice.

He leaned around the woman to stare up the church steps at the man speaking. It *was* that Patrick Henry. It was Jerry!

Sam couldn't believe it. What was Jerry doing in Williamsburg? Did he perform as Patrick Henry all over the world? This was terrible.

Derek looked nervous, too. He started to leave, pulling Sam's arm behind him. They bumped into people on their way through the crowd, a mixture of tourists and actors blended together. Everything was a blur to Sam.

This had gone all wrong.

"Sorry," said Derek, as he knocked into a man in black boots. "Excuse me," he called to another.

A voice boomed down into the crowd. "Young men, why do you leave in such haste from our gathering? Are you not interested to learn about the independence that is soon to be declared for us all in Philadelphia?"

It was Jerry's voice, and he was speaking to them! They'd caused too much commotion trying to get out of the crowd.

One of the characters in front of them put his hand on Sam's shoulder and pointed. "Mr. Henry is speaking to you, lad."

Sam stopped his pushing and stood still, the man's hand resting on his shoulder. It reminded him of when Jerry stopped him in the basement of the church. Slowly, he turned and looked up through the crowd at Jerry.

"Surely you aren't a spy for the British, seeking to infiltrate our assembly, are you?" Jerry shouted while the crowd around him laughed.

Jerry turned his glance down, seeing Sam's face for the first time. Immediately his expression turned serious. Sam knew Jerry had recognized him when his eyes narrowed and his mouth drew tight.

For a moment, Jerry stood silently.

Sam imagined he was deciding how to play this unexpected twist in the colonial drama. He was probably as surprised to see Sam in Williamsburg as Sam was to see him. Thankfully, Jerry's options were limited in front of all these people.

"Sorry, we have to go!" shouted Derek. He pulled Sam back to reality and out of the crowd.

Jerry recovered from his surprise and quickly slipped back into his Patrick Henry character. "Perhaps I was mistaken. These are not British spies, but simply youths who are late for their mother's lunch!" He watched the boys hustle across the street as the crowd chuckled, waiting for the rest of the program to continue.

Sam couldn't breathe. He felt like he was back at St. John's Church. This whole week was one bad reenactment of fear. Why did he keep getting himself in these situations?

The boys ran over to Mom and Dad who had finally finished with basket weaving. Now they were watching a woman describe how vegetables were grown in a colonial garden.

Sam tugged on his dad's sleeve and tried to talk to him. "Dad," he panted, out of breath.

"Why have you guys been running? You need to take it easy. There's going to be a lot of walking today and you're not going to make it at this rate."

"We...we have to tell you something!" Sam tried to say in between breaths.

Derek interrupted before Sam could say any more. "Can we take a break and go to Aunt Karen's? We're starving, and you said we'd go there for lunch."

Derek shot Sam a look that told him to be quiet.

Mom finished with the vegetable lady and came over to them. "You boys *want* to visit Aunt Karen? I swear I can't figure you out these days." She checked her watch and then looked at Dad. "Well, it is past lunch time. I suppose we could take a break."

The boys nodded in quick agreement and followed their parents back to the car.

It was only a few minutes' drive to Aunt Karen's house, but Sam didn't want to talk. In his mind, all he could see were Jerry's beady eyes. They were staring at him. It was like he had some kind of evil mind-lock, and Sam couldn't tear away. Sam would never have suggested coming to Williamsburg if he had known Jerry would be here, too. He wondered if this trip was one mistake too many. They were sure starting to pile up.

TWELVE

THE HUNT

Once the family arrived at Great-Aunt Karen's house, the boys suffered through the requisite hellos and hugs. Aunt Karen was eighty-five years old. She was their grandma's sister, or something like that, Mom had said. They listened to the old woman gush over how much they'd grown and resembled their father.

After a few minutes, Mom got their lunch requests, and the boys retreated to the back porch. Sam stared off into the row of green hedges that separated Aunt Karen's backyard from the neighbors'. His head was spinning again.

"Of all the places that we had to go," moaned Sam, "we pick the exact place where HE is! What are the chances of that?"

"Probably greater than most. We *did* go to another

historic colonial site where they have reenactments," Derek pointed out.

Sam lay back on the patio with his hand over his face. "Ugh! What are we going to do?"

The sliding door to the patio squeaked open. Mom stepped out carrying her cell phone.

"Sam, you have a phone call."

"I do?" Sam sat up in surprise. Who in the world would be calling him here? He thought of Jerry. Maybe he'd tracked Sam down. Maybe Jerry had *his* phone number! Was he calling to tell Sam he was dead meat?

"It's Caitlin Murphy," smiled Mom as she handed him the phone.

Derek smirked and made a kissing face. "Do you need some privacy?" he teased, as he followed Mom into the house.

Sam waved him off and put the phone up to his ear. "Caitlin?"

"Hi, Sam. Sorry to bother you with your family, but I just had to talk to you some more about this mystery. Are you in Williamsburg?"

"Yeah, we're here. How did you get my mom's cell phone number?" Sam asked.

"Oh, well, my mom asked Brandon's mom. She had it from the minutes of the PTA board meeting last week. See, they print everyone's contact numbers at the bottom…"

"Never mind," said Sam, interrupting her before she kept going on forever. "It doesn't matter. What's up?"

"Well, first of all, did you find the Wythe House? Was there anything in his study that matched the letter or the key?"

"Yeah, we found the house and went on a tour," said Sam. "Derek and I are pretty sure that the key we have is some kind of slide that fits into his solar microscope. It shines onto the wall like an overhead projector. It may even have a secret message."

"A solar microscope, very interesting! It actually fits, given his Enlightenment philosophy – using light and your senses and all."

"Right, that's what the tour guide said." Sam was surprised by her knowledge. It was impressive, even for Caitlin. "How did you know that?"

"I told you, I've been doing a lot of research," she answered. "So what are you going to do next? Did you tell your parents?"

"Derek wants to sneak back into the house so we can try the key in the microscope. And no, we haven't told our parents yet, but I think we should. This is all getting too dangerous." Sam told Caitlin how they'd run into Jerry at the assembly in town.

"Well, I have to confess something," Caitlin said quietly. "I did tell my parents."

"You what?" cried Sam. "Caitlin, tell me you didn't."

"Okay, I didn't."

"Wait, but you just said you did!"

"Well, sort of," she continued. "I told them we had found some old papers that looked important, and that you guys were in Williamsburg looking for clues. I kind of made it sound like it was for a research project for Mrs. H."

"Oh," said Sam, considering her answer. "Well, I guess that won't hurt anything." He didn't think that he'd ever heard Caitlin call their teacher Mrs. H before. It had always been "Mrs. Haperwink." Maybe she was loosening up.

She wasn't done. "*And* I kind of am in the car right now with them driving to Williamsburg."

"You're what?" shouted Sam.

Derek walked back onto the porch with a questioning look. Sam closed his eyes and just shook his head. This was getting out of hand.

He wrote down Caitlin's parents' cell phone number and gave her Aunt Karen's number. They agreed to try to meet up later that afternoon by the historic area. He didn't like the idea of her parents knowing anything before his own parents did. Still, her research had been really helpful. Maybe it would be okay to have her on the hunt, too.

Sam caught himself thinking that she didn't even seem quite as annoying as usual. All this mystery stuff must be messing with his brain.

Dad walked out onto the porch. "Boys, your Mom and I are going to head over to the chapel for a little while to visit the place where we got married. We might take a walk through the campus afterwards. Do you guys want to come along or stay here with Aunt Karen?"

"We'll stay here," Derek blurted out before Sam could answer. "Sam said he's feeling tired, and I was going to talk to Aunt Karen about her antiques."

Dad gave Derek a look that said he knew that he was up to something. Mom was waiting by the front door, though, so he didn't take the time to argue.

Once Dad had left, Derek leaped up from his chair. "This is perfect! Now we can give Aunt Karen the slip and head back over to the Wythe House. Caitlin can meet us there."

They went back into the house, carefully navigating around a sea of antique furniture, glass vases, and other valuables.

"Where is she?" asked Derek, glancing around the room.

"I don't know," said Sam. "Maybe she's taking a nap. Old people do that sometimes." He walked over to a glass door that was cracked open and peered through. "Aunt Karen?"

Derek pushed past Sam through the doorway. "See anything?"

"No, it's too dark."

Sam slipped around his brother and into the room. The windows were covered by wooden blinds, allowing only a faint light to trickle in from the edges. He scanned the walls. They were filled with picture frames of all shapes and sizes. One caught his eye, so he walked up to the wall to check it out. A faded black-and-white photograph showed a young girl standing under a tree in front of a square brick house.

"Look, Derek, isn't that the Wythe House?"

Derek inched past a desk so he could stand next to Sam. "Whoa, I think you're right. It looks about the same as it does now. I wonder who that girl is? She kind of looks like Mom."

"That's me, Sweetie."

The boys jumped at the voice. When they whirled around, they noticed Aunt Karen sitting in a rocking chair on the far side of the darkened room.

"Oh my gosh," exclaimed Derek, grabbing his chest. "You almost gave me a heart attack, Aunt Karen!"

"Don't scare us like that!" said Sam, exhaling in relief.

The old woman let out a cackle. She tapped her cane against a table and motioned for them to come over.

"That's you in the picture?" asked Sam.

"You betcha," answered the old woman. "My daddy took that picture after church on my tenth birthday.

Seems like it was just yesterday. I sure was a looker, wasn't I?"

"Uh, yeah," answered Sam, not really sure what she meant. He'd have to ask Caitlin.

"Did you visit the Wythe House?" asked Derek. "We saw it this morning. There are all kinds of cool instruments up in the study."

"Ah, yes," replied Aunt Karen, gazing up at the picture. "George Wythe was a famous teacher. He loved Thomas Jefferson like a son. They were both quite learned men and full of all kinds of interesting ideas and inventions. Did you know that George Wythe designed the Virginia State Seal?"

"Is that like a sea lion?" asked Derek.

Sam rolled his eyes and smacked his brother. Aunt Karen's mouth was turned up in a slight smirk. Sam wasn't sure if she actually got Derek's lame joke or if that was just how old ladies' faces looked.

"We think he may have hidden a secret document somewhere in the house. It's something Thomas Jefferson gave him," Sam blurted out. With all the excitement, he couldn't help himself.

"Sam!" Derek elbowed his brother, giving him the evil eye to keep his mouth shut.

"What?" asked Sam. He was getting tired of all these secrets. Besides, what could Aunt Karen do? She probably wouldn't even remember having this conversation after they left.

"Is that right?" said Aunt Karen. "How exciting for you boys. Many of the Founding Fathers were experts in codes, symbols, and various cyphers. Did you know that?"

Interesting, thought Sam. That could explain why Wythe would create such an elaborate and clever way to keep things hidden. It was cool, but it certainly would have been easier if he'd just stuck something in a drawer. Although if Wythe had done that, Sam realized, there would be no mystery for them to solve. The document wouldn't have stayed so well hidden for over 200 years.

"Thanks for telling us," Derek said.

The old woman sat silently in her chair, not moving or making a sound.

"Aunt Karen?" Sam leaned over and saw that her eyes were closed.

"Is she dead?" asked Derek. This was too weird. He motioned to the door as if to say they should get going.

"Would you boys like something to eat?" Aunt Karen opened her eyes, springing back to life.

Old people sure could be creepy.

The boys thanked Aunt Karen for passing along the information and said they were headed back to the Wythe House. She pointed them in the direction of the Historic Area. Since she lived right in town, it was only a matter of cutting through a few lawns and parking lots until they saw the old wooden fences dead ahead.

As they proceeded up Duke of Gloucester Street, Sam got even more nervous. On the way, he'd tried to explain to Derek that Jerry could be waiting for them. He insisted they stay close to the buildings rather than march down the middle of the street. This would make it harder for Jerry to spot them. Sam half expected Jerry to jump out at them from behind every building.

As they walked past the stocks, the Wythe House came into view.

"Sam!" a voice called out across the street.

Startled, Sam nearly fell into a horse trough that was full of water. He recovered enough to see a figure walking toward them in the sunlight.

"Hey, Caitlin. Fancy meeting you here."

"Hi, Derek." Caitlin looked at Sam leaning against the water trough. "What's the matter, Sam? You look like you saw a ghost!"

"The ghost of Patrick Henry!" laughed Derek. "He's worried that Jerry is going to grab him."

"For good reason," replied Sam, standing up straight. "He *is* here, you know." He didn't understand why no one else was taking it seriously.

"Where are your parents, Caitlin?" asked Derek.

"I, uh, told them I was going on a tour with your family," she confessed. "Where are *your* parents?"

Sam thought about how they'd lied to Mom and Dad. He was excited to find things on their own, but he knew they shouldn't be lying.

"They're busy at the chapel reliving their wedding vows," said Derek. "They think we're at Aunt Karen's. But as long as we do this quickly, we should be able to beat them home. You can call your parents from there."

"Okay, well what are we waiting for?" asked Caitlin. "Let's go see the Wythe House!"

THIRTEEN

THE SOLAR MICROSCOPE

The three kids stood under an oak tree up the street from the Wythe House. They eyed the building as if they were a couple of advance scouts for General Washington's army. Derek filled Caitlin in on his plan for getting back to the study and the solar microscope.

When it looked like no one was watching, Derek led them behind the Wythe House, sneaking past the stable and kitchen outbuildings next to the gardens. The grounds seemed empty in the late afternoon, so they walked straight up the path to the back of the house. Derek pulled at the door, but it was locked.

"Okay, it's locked. Let's go," urged Sam.

Caitlin moved off the stairs and pointed to a short window near the ground. It was covered by wide white slats.

"What about down there?" she suggested. "Is that the basement? Maybe we could we get in there."

"Good idea!" said Derek. They followed him to the side of the house where several stone steps led down to an old black door. A thick chain hung loose from an open lock.

Sam gave Caitlin an annoyed glance. It *was* a good idea, but he wished they would just leave.

Derek pulled at the door. It slowly creaked open. Poking his head through, he waved that the coast was clear.

Inside, they saw what looked like an open storage room with closets. Wooden boxes and extra furnishings lay strewn in the corners. One of the walls contained a hefty stone fireplace. The ceiling was a series of huge wooden beams holding up the floor above them. The beams were dark brown and roughly sawn, like they were from an old barn. It reminded him of the basement at St. John's Church.

"Here are the stairs," called Caitlin from around the corner.

Together they scaled the stairs, cracking open the door at the top. Sam peered around Derek's head and recognized the bright blue wallpaper. They were in the hallway on the first floor. They paused to listen for the tour guide walking around, but they didn't hear anything.

Derek waved them forward, and they scrambled into the hall, tiptoeing up the stairway to George Wythe's study.

When they entered the room, the boys went quickly over to the window. The solar microscope was no longer fastened onto the shutter. They looked around the table and found it lying among the other instruments.

"Do you remember how to put it back on the shutter?" Caitlin asked Sam.

"I think so," he replied, carefully picking up the old device. He placed it through the hole in the shutter as he'd seen their tour guide do earlier.

Caitlin listened at the door for anyone coming up the stairs. They agreed that if anyone caught them, they would act like they were lost from a tour. That wouldn't be so easy if they were caught fooling with the solar microscope. They'd just have to wing it.

Derek helped adjust the clamps, and soon the microscope was held firm against the shutter.

"I don't know if this is exactly right, but it should work for now," said Derek. "Sam, put the key into the slide spot and cross your fingers."

Sam took the rectangular piece out of his pocket and slid it between the metal holders. He tried to remember how the tour guide had placed the glass flea slide. When it seemed secure, Sam stepped back and looked at the wall.

Nothing happened.

"What's wrong? I put our key slide in just like he did before," explained Sam. After all this, could they have the wrong device? Was it all just a wild goose chase?

Caitlin looked over from the doorway. "Did you adjust the lens?"

"Oh, right," replied Sam. He should have thought of that. He looked closely at the microscope. If he could only figure out which piece adjusted the lens.

"Here, let me try," said Caitlin, suddenly standing next to him. "My dad has a microscope at home. Maybe it works the same way."

She tilted the round piece of glass a bit higher to catch the late-day sun and then turned a delicate looking dial.

Sam looked up at the wall and began to see the round spotlight. But was there anything inside it? Caitlin turned the dial some more, and he began to see some lines.

"Can you close those other shutters?" Caitlin pointed to the window on the far wall. "I think it'll work better if the room's really dark."

Sam went over and pulled the hinged shutters closed. They let out a loud creak as they banged shut against the window.

"Sam! Be quiet about it," scolded Derek.

Sam hoped that no one had heard the noise from outside. As the room grew darker, the round light on the wall became more prominent. Caitlin gave the dial one more turn.

"Look at that!" said Sam, running over to the wall. He saw a series of dark squares and lines.

"What is it?" asked Derek, stepping further back to get a wider look. "Are those shapes?"

"I think it's…a map," said Caitlin, moving from the microscope to the wall. "Look, these boxes are buildings, and this outside mark is like a fence. Maybe it marks off a piece of property. And what are these little words on this big rectangle?" She moved up close and tried to read.

"W…H…, no that's a Y….W, Y, T…Wythe, it says Wythe! Is it the Wythe House? Maybe a map of the Wythe House property? It has to be!"

"Oh yeah," said Derek. "You're right. See, here's the servant's house that we were in front of this morning. Back here are the gardens, and here are the stables."

"And look!" added Sam. "There's an 'X'! X marks the spot, right? It looks like the back corner of the garden. That must be where Jefferson's copy of the Declaration is buried! Sweet!"

They'd done it! They'd figured out the mystery!

As Sam gave Derek a big high five, another shadow filled the wall next to the spotlight.

"Very impressive!" said a voice booming from the hallway.

Sam's heart stopped. He knew that voice too well.

He turned and saw Jerry standing in the doorway. Memories of being trapped in the basement on Church Hill flooded his mind.

"What do you want? Leave us alone!" he cried.

"I have to say, I never would have expected a couple of kids to figure out the riddle before me," Jerry said. "And look, you brought a little friend. Were you involved in this caper too, young lady? I'll bet you are the brains behind the operation."

"I don't know who you think you are, but we found this secret, not you," responded Caitlin in a fiery voice. "We're going to leave now, and then we're going to tell the police and the head of Colonial Williamsburg what we found."

"And the FBI!" shouted Derek.

Sam looked up at the man. He had forgotten how big and tall he was. Sam pictured Jerry squeezing the air out of him in a giant bear hug.

"Oh, I have to disagree with you," Jerry laughed. "It's not your secret. It's mine. I've been searching for this much longer than you have. If this one here," he pointed down at Sam, "hadn't stumbled upon the couple of idiots that were working for me over at the church, you'd never have known about my little treasure."

He walked over and pulled the key slide out of the microscope. "I appreciate you making all the noise with the shutter. I may not have found you up here otherwise."

Sam shook his head. He should have been more careful with the shutter.

"And I don't think you're going to be telling anyone about this, either," Jerry added in an even deeper voice than usual. His hand reached inside his fancy coat.

Sam couldn't believe his eyes when he saw Jerry holding a gun! It was one of those old revolver types from colonial times. Was that real or just a prop for the show? It was hard to tell, but Sam wasn't about to find out. He pictured himself lying on the floor in George Wythe's study, crying out that he'd been murdered, just like poor George!

"Let's go," Jerry barked. "All of you, down the stairs!"

Derek seemed like he was thinking about trying to be the hero. Sam tried to get his attention and shook his head. Caitlin had a look on her face that Sam had never seen before. She was staring at the revolver, but he couldn't tell whether she was scared to death or just really mad. Sam took her hand and they followed Derek out of the room.

Jerry followed behind them holding the gun in one hand and the key he'd taken out of the microscope in the other. He marched them all the way down to the basement, ordering them against the wall next to the big fireplace.

"What are you going to do to us?" Derek demanded.

"Our parents know where we are. They'll be looking for us any minute!"

Sam started to feel even worse about lying now. He realized that Mom and Dad had no idea where they were. He'd told Aunt Karen, but who knows if she remembered what they'd said. And now Caitlin was mixed up in this, too.

"You kids are going to take a little time off from your snooping so I can have some peace and quiet. Just sit tight and relax. By the time they find you in the morning, I'll be long gone. Nighty-night!"

FOURTEEN

THE BASEMENT

T he heavy door slammed shut. They heard the lock turn and a chain jingled on the door. Sam could picture Jerry looping the thick black chain through the latch. There was no way they could get out now.

As Jerry's shoes clackety-clacked up the stone steps, a different voice called out. "Hello, Jerry."

Sam recognized it as their tour guide from earlier.

"I was just coming to lock up for the day, but I see that you already have. Is everything squared away in there?"

Sam jumped at the sound of the other voice. All the kids started yelling as loud as they could.

"Help! Down here!" but their voices were drowned out by a thunderous boom. The cannons were going off at the Governor's Palace again. When the explosions ended, there were no more voices outside. The tour guide must have left.

When they realized their yelling wasn't getting them anywhere, Sam, Derek and Caitlin rested silently against the cold stone wall.

Sam looked up at the wooden ceiling beams and moaned. "What are we going to do?"

"I don't think anyone is coming back here until the morning," said Caitlin. "That cannon means that tours are done for the day and the buildings are all closing."

Derek stood up and walked around the room. "Okay, let's not panic! We'll find a way out of this. Sam, do you remember last summer when I got stuck in the cave with the lost coins? I started to get nervous and freaked out. I thought I was going to die in that cave. It was awful."

"Wow, thanks for the pep talk, Derek," said Sam. "You should be a motivational speaker. Are you trying to make us feel even worse?"

"No, listen. I'm not done. We can't let ourselves get down. I found a way out of that, and we'll find a way out of this, too. We just have to think. Maybe there's another exit out of here."

"That's not likely, Derek," sighed Sam. He was starting to feel helpless.

"I think Derek's right," said Caitlin. "Maybe there is some other way out of here. My research said George

Washington also used this house for a short time. It was his headquarters for the colonial army during the revolution. Maybe there *is* a secret escape route."

Sam looked out the small window near the ceiling and could tell it would be dark soon. He pictured spending the night on the cold floor in the old house. A chill ran down his spine.

He walked over to the big stone fireplace, wishing there was a fire going to keep them warm. He leaned in and peered up at the chimney. Maybe they could climb out that way? When he saw that it was bricked off, he slumped down on the floor in defeat.

"I wonder where Jerry is now," said Caitlin.

"He's probably back in the gardens digging up the Declaration at the spot on the map," answered Derek. "Jefferson's letter said it was lying in a shallow grave, right? That sounds like it was buried."

Sam leaned his head against the fireplace. "I just want to get out of here!" he yelled and kicked the stone with his foot in frustration. "Ouch!" he moaned even louder. His toe started throbbing.

"Smooth, Sam," said Derek. "Let's try not to hurt ourselves. We've got enough trouble as it is."

"Are you okay, Sam?" asked Caitlin.

"Yeah, sorry, that was dumb," he answered. "I just wanted to…" He didn't finish his sentence because he looked at the side of the fireplace and saw that a piece of the stone had chipped away. There was an opening about the size of a brick in the side of the fireplace.

"Look at that!" Sam exclaimed.

Derek and Caitlin walked over to the fireplace and looked where Sam was pointing.

"No way!" shouted Derek. "Is that an opening? Maybe it really *is* a secret passage?"

"Look there," pointed Caitlin, "what are those letters etched into the stone?"

"G.W.," read Sam. "George Wythe?"

"Or it could be George Washington," said Caitlin. "Maybe it's a secret escape tunnel from the revolution. They could have needed one to get the general out of the house."

"I don't care whose initials they are," said Derek. "Move out of the way. We have to see if that hole opens any further and see where it leads. Maybe we just found our way out of here."

Derek gave the side of the fireplace his best karate kick. Lo and behold, another chunk of stone fell away. A dark empty space had opened up behind it. After a few more kicks, he'd cleared an opening large enough for them to crawl through.

Sam leaned his head into the passage and tried to look around, but it was pitch black. He couldn't see a thing. "I wish we had a flashlight or something. There's no telling what's in there or where it leads."

"We don't have time to worry about that," answered Derek. "We'll just have to risk it. Come on!"

Derek held his hand out in front of him, feeling his path as he climbed through the hole. He inched forward a few steps and then called back to the others. "There's stairs going down. They must lead under the house. Come on, just be careful."

Sam and Caitlin followed, carefully descending the stone staircase. They walked single-file along the narrow passageway in the darkness, holding hands so they didn't get separated. At the bottom of the stairs the ceiling dropped low, and they had to lean over to walk.

Sam imagined General George Washington and George Wythe sneaking through the passageway with a candle held out in front of them. Maybe the British had been in the house upstairs and a fast horse had been waiting by the trees. They must have been nervous. He could relate to that.

Sam wished he had a candle now.

They moved along the passage a bit at a time. Derek kept testing the floor in front of them with his hand to make sure they didn't smack into a wall or fall into a hole.

The human chain stopped suddenly. "What's the matter?" Sam called up to Derek.

"There's a wall here. It's a dead end."

"No! That can't be," Sam cried. "Why would anyone build a passage like this that leads to nowhere? It doesn't make any sense!"

"Maybe it used to lead somewhere and they closed it off," sighed Derek in frustration. "I guess we need to turn around."

"Wait," said Caitlin. "What if it does lead somewhere?"

"Caitlin, I know you're smart and all," answered Derek, "but I told you there's a stone wall here. It's a dead end, we're stuck."

"I know, but what if it doesn't keep going straight. What if it goes up?"

"I don't feel any stairs," said Derek.

"What if there is something else..." She started feeling the stone above them with her hands. "Something like this!"

Sam reached his hand up and was surprised to feel a section in the ceiling made of wood. It felt like a door! They all moved underneath the wood section, pushing with their hands as hard as they could. The boards inched up, but then smacked right back down against the stone.

"I think it's a trap door, but something's on top of it," said Sam. "Let's try it another way." He moved them back into position. This time they pushed using their legs and tried to stand up in the small passage, the boards against their shoulders. The door eased up a few inches again until they heard something move above them. There was a loud crash. All at once the boards came free and the door flung open.

"All right!" they all cheered.

FIFTEEN

THE STABLE

D erek climbed up through the trapdoor, reaching down to help Sam and Caitlin. They peered around the dimly lit room. It was the size of a large kitchen, but it was hard to see. There were large wooden dividers separating the room along one wall. A tall wooden barrel lay turned over on its side next to the opening they'd crawled through. It must have been sitting on top of the trapdoor before they knocked it over.

"What is this place?" asked Sam. He walked around the room slowly, his hand out in front of him so he didn't crash into anything.

"I think it's the stable behind the Wythe House," said Derek. "Remember, we walked past it this morning after the tour. The gardens are over there." He pointed out the door.

Sam crept over to the open door and surveyed the

courtyard. It was mostly dark now, making it tough to see. The Wythe House loomed in a large dark shadow to their left. Its twin brick chimneys stuck out high above the roofline on both sides like the horns on a bull. The gardens stretched in front of them, and another outbuilding was to their right. Next to that was an over-sized white birdhouse on poles. It had dozens of small holes in the side that were like tiny caverns on the side of a cliff-face. Sam thought he remembered the tour guide saying it was a pigeon house.

"I don't see anyone," Sam whispered back to the others.

"Okay, then let's get out of here!" Derek headed for the doorway.

"Wait!" hissed Sam. "We don't know where Jerry is. He could be right out there!"

Caitlin crouched next to Sam in the doorway as they peered out into the yard again. A shadow shifted behind the gardens.

Sam held his hand up. "Look, over there!"

In the far corner of the garden, a faint light flickered behind the outline of a figure moving back and forth.

Sam listened carefully. He heard a shovel hitting dirt.

"It's him," whispered Sam. "It has to be."

"He's digging up the Declaration," said Caitlin. "We can't let him get away with that. It's such an important piece of history. Who knows what he'll do with it?"

Sam gulped and turned back into the stables. His heart was beating fast. He looked for Derek, but he was gone.

"Derek!" Why did his brother always have to go running off?

"I'm up here," came a voice above them.

They looked up and saw Derek's head sticking out of the hayloft. There was a wooden ladder near the wall that led up to the loft in the stable.

"What are you *doing*?" scolded Sam.

"Looking around. Come on up here, I've got a plan."

Sam had that same bad feeling again that often accompanied Derek's plans. They scrambled up the ladder, crouching next to Derek on the wooden boards. He was perched by a small door that looked like it was once used to load hay into the loft from the outside. At the top of the door was a pulley mounted to a beam. A thick rope hung down to the ground.

Derek filled them in on his plan. "Okay, Jerry's over there in the corner of the garden. Caitlin, do you think you can run fast?"

"Sure, I think so."

"Great," said Derek. "You'll be the diversion to get Jerry's attention. Once he spots you, run around to the front of the Wythe House. See if you can find a security guard or someone in town and bring help fast.

"While you're running, Sam and I will lure Jerry into

129

the stable and try to lock him in one of the stalls. That should hold him until you get back with help."

It wasn't exactly a foolproof plan, thought Sam, but it was better than nothing.

They snuck around the corner of the stable in the darkness, hugging the border of the gardens. They kept low behind the plantings and bushes to stay out of Jerry's sight. As they drew closer, they could see him digging in one of the flowerbeds a few yards off the path. Several mounds of dirt were scattered around him, as though he'd tried a few different spots without success.

They crept up behind the giant birdhouse and sat silently for a few moments, watching him dig. He seemed to be getting agitated and was muttering to himself. The evening was still except for the rhythmic sound of his shovel smacking into the dirt.

All of a sudden, they heard the shovel hit something wooden. Caitlin gasped and grabbed onto Sam's arm. "We have to do something!"

They watched Jerry reach into the hole and pull out what seemed to be a wooden crate. It wasn't a huge box, but about the size of a large picture frame. Sam could almost make out Jerry's greedy grin as he hauled the crate up.

Derek leaned in close to them and whispered. "Now's our chance."

Caitlin inched her leg back to prepare for her sprint

to the house. Instead, she kicked one of the giant bird-house poles. As she did, dozens of birds came to life, fluttering out of the house with a great swoosh. Caitlin let out a scream and covered her head with her arms as they flew past.

The commotion drew Jerry's attention. He stood up and saw Caitlin next to the birdhouse. "Hey! How did you get out of there?" he bellowed. "Get over here!" He dropped the crate and started running toward them.

This wasn't how the plan was supposed to go. Caitlin was meant to be up by the house when she distracted him so that she could get away easily. Jerry was too close!

"Run, Caitlin!" shouted Sam, springing up from his hiding place.

As Caitlin sprinted up the path toward the house, Sam ran toward the stable with Jerry hot on his trail. Derek hadn't moved from the shadows yet, so when Jerry ran past, Derek stuck out his leg. The big man went sprawling through the air. He flew smack into the bird-house, which came toppling down on him with a crash. Derek leaped up and followed Sam to the stable as Jerry lay stunned beneath the birdhouse.

Sam looked across the garden and saw Caitlin round the corner of the house toward the street. He was relieved that she was in the clear and on the way to get help. He was determined to beat Jerry once and for all. They'd already outsmarted him by finding the letter, and now they were doing it again.

Sam and Derek reached the stable just as Jerry was rising to his feet. He was like a Frankenstein monster that just wouldn't stay down. Sam hustled through the stable door and up the ladder into the hayloft. There was no time to lock Jerry in a stall now; they'd just have to outrun him.

Derek paused at the doorway. "Hey Jerry," he called, "I still have your phone number!" Then he scrambled up the ladder behind Sam.

Jerry just growled as he lumbered after them. He ran into the stable, scanning the dark room.

"Up here, Jerry!" shouted Sam from the hayloft.

As Jerry's heavy footsteps clanged up the ladder, Sam and Derek ran to the hayloft door.

Derek grabbed the rope that was on the pulley and jumped down, riding it like a zip line. "Come on, Sam!" he called from below.

When Sam saw Jerry reach the top of the ladder, he turned to grab the rope, but his foot caught on a loose board and he fell down.

"Aaaahh!" Sam shrieked, as Jerry moved toward him.

Sam scrambled to his feet and reached out for the rope. He looked down at the ground and gulped. He didn't like heights, but he didn't like Jerry even more. He grabbed onto the rope, closed his eyes and jumped, bracing for the landing. He didn't fall downward, though, he was hung up on something. He opened his eyes and saw that Jerry had grabbed the corner of his jacket.

"Gotcha, kid!" Jerry laughed, tugging on Sam's jacket to reel him back into the hayloft.

"Sam, come on!" screamed Derek again. He pulled the rope from the bottom to help free Sam from Jerry's grasp.

Sam strained with all of his might against Jerry's grip, trying to wriggle out of his jacket.

"You're not getting loose this time!" grunted Jerry, moving closer. He let go of the side of the door with his other hand and reached out to pull on Sam's arm.

As he did, Sam lifted his leg and delivered a solid kick to the big man's knee, the same one he'd hit with the rock in the church. Thrown off balance by the unexpected kick, Jerry loosened his grip on Sam's jacket. Sam pulled loose and slid down the side of the barn on the rope, landing next to Derek.

In the hayloft, Jerry was left holding nothing but air. His momentum carried him out the door. He bashed his head on the beam that held the rope pulley and fell to the ground. Sam and Derek leaped out of the way as Jerry landed near them on a pile of hay bales.

Sam picked himself up off the ground and looked at Jerry. He wasn't moving. Sam wondered if the hay had broken his fall or if he had broken his neck.

"Is he dead?"

Derek put his hand on Jerry's chest. "No, I feel him breathing. He must have knocked himself out on that beam."

"What should we do? He might wake up soon, and he's going to be angrier than ever!" said Sam.

"Wait here, I have an idea!" Derek ran into the stable and came out pushing an old wooden cart. "Here, we can roll him into this." He pulled the cart up next to Jerry. "Help me move him."

With Sam on one side of Jerry's body and Derek on the other, they heaved him off the hay bales. Gravity helped him topple into the cart.

"Ouch!" grimaced Sam, as Jerry's head bounced into the cart. "That's gonna leave a mark.

"Okay, so what do we do with him now?"

"Help me push! We'll take him around to the front of the house," answered Derek.

They each picked up a handle and turned the wagon toward the path. It wasn't easy since Jerry was so heavy, but the wheels helped carry the load. Soon they pulled it around the house and out to the road.

Sam peered nervously over the man's body to see if his eyes were open. He imagined Jerry leaping out of the cart and grabbing him again.

"Let's bring him over here." Derek pointed toward the street corner.

Sam looked across the dark street in the moonlight and saw what Derek was pointing to. For the first time in a while, he smiled. "Oh yeah!" he said under his breath.

The boys wheeled the cart up to the corner next to the old wooden stocks they'd passed earlier in the day. The heavy beams worked on a hinge, so Derek ran over and opened the top piece.

They rolled Jerry onto his back and then heaved the cart up. Jerry spilled forward and hung over the wooden supports. They pulled his big arms over the bottom beam and his head fell into place in the center notch.

Derek pulled the top piece back down and fastened the latch. "Got him!"

"Are you sure he can't get loose?" worried Sam. "Those stocks are pretty old. Maybe he can break out."

"No way." Derek slapped the sturdy wood beam with his hand. "This thing is solid.

"Now, for the wake-up call!" Derek walked over to the horse trough next to the fence, pulling out a bucket of water. He carried it over to the stocks and dumped it on Jerry's head. "Wakey wakey, Jerry!"

Jerry's head moved with a jerk, and he began coughing under the water. He let out a moan and opened his eyes. He tried to get up, but quickly realized he was locked in tight.

"What the..." he shouted and started shaking the

beams with all his might. The stocks jiggled, but held firm.

"You're not going anywhere, Jerry!" taunted Derek.

Jerry glared up at them with his evil eyes and grunted. Then he put his head down in defeat and moaned.

Derek reached over and gave Sam a high five in the cool night air. "We did it!" he exclaimed.

Sam smiled. He finally had no worries of Jerry coming for him. He looked at the big man bent over in the wooden restraints.

"I'll bet liberty is sounding pretty good right now, huh, Jerry?" laughed Sam.

SIXTEEN

THE CRATE

"Sam! Derek!" a voice called from up the street. The boys looked up and saw a group of flashlights bouncing toward them from across the darkness. Night had fully set in, so the boys couldn't make out who it was.

One light pulled ahead of the others, and soon Caitlin was standing next to them. She looked in amazement at Jerry trapped in the stocks. The crowd behind her turned out to be Mom, Dad, and another couple who Sam figured must be Caitlin's parents. Next to them were two men in uniform whom he didn't recognize.

"Are you hurt?" asked Mom, rushing over and holding their faces up to the light for inspection. She sighed in relief to see them standing there safely.

"Boys, what have you gotten into this time?" asked Dad. In the darkness, Sam couldn't tell if he was really mad or just concerned. "Aunt Karen told us that you might be over by the Wythe House. We ran into Caitlin on our way."

"Will someone please get me out of here?" shouted Jerry from the stocks. "These crazy kids attacked me and locked me in here while I was unconscious! This is outrageous. I'll be pressing charges!"

The two men in uniform stepped forward, shining their flashlights on the stocks. One man had a patch on his jacket that said *Colonial Williamsburg Security*. The other's man's patch said *Town of Williamsburg Police*.

"Mr. Milburn, is that you?" the security guard asked.

"Yes, it's me!" Jerry bellowed, "Now get me out of here!"

The police officer nodded. They unlatched the bolt and raised the top wooden bar that was holding Jerry down.

"No, don't let him out of there!" shouted Sam. "He's gonna come after us again!"

"Take it easy, boys," the police officer responded. "No one is going anywhere."

The security guard pulled Jerry from the stocks, and he wobbled onto the sidewalk.

Sam's confidence started to waver. He hadn't considered that they may have done something illegal by trapping Jerry in there. What if no one believed them? Jerry was a trusted local actor in Williamsburg and Richmond. Maybe they would believe *him* instead!

The police officer turned to Sam and Derek. "The young lady filled us in on the basics of what happened." He motioned to Caitlin. "But why don't you explain the rest of it."

Sam felt better. Thank goodness for Caitlin.

Derek told everyone how Jerry had chased them through the stable and knocked himself out on the wooden beam. He explained that they had put him in the stocks because it was the only way they could keep Jerry from escaping or killing them.

"That's all preposterous!" Jerry barked, rising to his feet. "Why would I try to hurt these kids? I'm a classically trained actor. My Patrick Henry portrayal earned me seven consecutive Virginia Golden Musket Awards!"

"Oh yeah? Well, we can prove it!" said Sam, gathering his courage. He'd had enough of Jerry. It made him mad to hear him claim to be innocent. He nodded to Derek.

"Right!" Derek continued, "Follow us!"

The boys led the way back around the building and through the gardens. The security guard walked with them while the police officer kept a hand on Jerry. They gathered around the back corner of the garden, shining the flashlight beams on all the piles of dirt where Jerry had been digging.

Sam looked around and found the crate lying next to a hole where Jerry had dropped it. He carried it over to the security guard.

"Here's the evidence. He was digging up this crate. We think it contains an early version of the Declaration of Independence. Thomas Jefferson gave it to George Wythe back in 1776."

Mom gasped as Sam described the contents of the crate. Everyone looked at each other, shocked by his announcement. Caitlin must not have told them exactly what Jerry had dug up.

Sam felt proud. He looked up to see Jerry's face.

"Hey, where'd he go?" Sam shouted. Jerry wasn't standing with the crowd. The police officer had leaned in to look at the crate and must have let go of Jerry's arm.

Everyone turned and shined their flashlights across the gardens.

"There he is!" shouted Caitlin, pointing behind the stable. The outline of a man could be seen shuffling along the wall.

"Freeze, Millburn!" yelled the officer, raising his gun.

Jerry skulked back into the light.

"You just earned yourself a night in lockup. You're under arrest." He marched over and slapped handcuffs on Jerry.

Modern-day stocks, thought Sam. Exactly where he belongs.

"All right!" shouted Derek.

Caitlin turned back to the crate. "We need to get this opened so we can see what's inside!"

"Not out here," answered the security guard. "Let's bring it over to the administration office. There's a table in the back room where we can work."

The guard led the way back along Duke of Gloucester Street to a slightly more modern looking brick building. The police officer brought Jerry along, holding his cuffed arm to prevent another escape.

As they entered the back room, another man was waiting at the table.

"I also took the liberty of calling the curator from the Virginia Museum to have a historical expert on hand."

Sam and Derek looked at each other and smiled. "Professor Evanshade!" they called in unison.

The security guard looked surprised. "You know each other?"

"Oh my golly!" the professor exclaimed. He said that when he got excited. "I should have guessed that you boys were in on this adventure!"

He turned to the security guard. "Jim, these two are some of my best junior investigators. They uncovered a magnificent collection of 1877 Indian Head cents last summer. It had been stolen from the museum back when I was a boy."

He turned to Caitlin. "But I have not met your friend."

Sam spoke up. "This is Caitlin. She's our research specialist!"

Caitlin looked over at him and smiled.

Dr. Evanshade shook Caitlin's hand. "A pleasure to meet you, young lady. I'm a big fan of your friends here."

"What are you doing here, Professor?" asked Derek.

"Oh, I work with the folks at Colonial Williamsburg from time to time when they need help authenticating an item. Jim here actually used to work security at my museum." He gestured to the security guard.

"Well, enough of this chit-chat. Let's get a look at your crate there!"

The professor lifted the crate onto the table. He opened a bag of equipment he'd brought with him, laying out several tools.

Sam thought Dr. Evanshade looked like a surgeon about to operate. Or maybe a car mechanic.

The professor selected a tool that looked like a small crowbar. Then he slowly loosened the side boards of the crate, one at a time.

"It's critical that we work carefully and methodically, children," he explained. "When something has been in the ground as long as this may have been, we never know what will crack or simply disintegrate when touched."

When both ends of the crate were removed, he gently lifted the top board. Everyone inched a step closer, leaning in toward the table. Sam turned around and noticed that even Mom and Dad were holding their breath.

Beneath the board was what seemed to be a cloth material. "Linen," explained the professor. "Quite common for storage in that period."

He pulled on a pair of latex gloves and tilted the light above the table slightly downward. He lifted the roll of fabric from the bottom of the crate. Slowly he began to turn it over and over, unrolling something inside. After a few more turns, the last stretch of linen pulled away.

Two thick sections of glass about the size of a newspaper page were what remained, held together with small clamps. It reminded Sam of the way that the solar microscope fitted onto the shutter in George Wythe's study.

Professor Evanshade carefully wiped the glass with a cloth. Then he set the glass sections onto the table for inspection. A yellowed sheet of paper was inside. The glass must have been pressed tight to preserve the paper from crumbling apart.

Dr. Evanshade selected a large magnifying glass with an extra light from his bag and leaned over the table. His head moved slowly from one side to the other. "Hmmm," he mumbled to himself. "Interesting."

"Well, is it the Declaration or what?" shouted Derek, unable to contain his curiosity any longer.

"Derek!" scolded Mom. "Wait until he's done. I'm sure he'll let us know."

Professor Evanshade stood up straight and lowered his magnifying glass. He turned around to the group and smiled. Even Jerry, standing with the police officer, looked filled with anticipation.

"Ladies and gentlemen," the professor began. "While we will certainly need to take this back to my laboratory at the museum for further testing, it appears to me that you have discovered an authentic document from the period of Thomas Jefferson in the late eighteenth century.

"From my quick read, the writing does look to be similar to the original Declaration of Independence. I suspect it is an early draft. There were several such copies generated for the different colonies to read back in 1776. However, only a few remain today, so this would be extremely rare. "

"All right!" shouted Derek.

"Sweet!" yelled Sam, as he high-fived his brother.

Caitlin let out a high-pitched shriek and gave Sam a hug.

Mom and Dad came over and put their hands on the boys' shoulders. "We're going to have another long talk about this when we get home, boys," said Dad.

Sam knew that his parents were angry at the way he and Derek had handled things, but he could tell they were impressed with their discovery. It's not every day that an important piece of American history is found buried in a flowerbed.

"Oh, I nearly forgot!" exclaimed Sam, reaching into

his backpack. "Here's the letter Thomas Jefferson wrote to George Wythe."

The professor looked it over. "Oh my golly, boys!"

Sam turned and pointed at Jerry who was leaning glumly against the wall. "And *he* has the key to the solar microscope that we used to find the spot in the garden."

Jerry reluctantly pulled the slide key out of his jacket and handed it over to the officer.

Sam walked up to Jerry. "There's one thing I still don't understand. How did you know that there was something hidden in St. John's Church? Did you have a map?"

Jerry's face grew red. "Why should I tell you? You have no idea how hard it was to find these documents!"

The police officer looked Jerry in the eye. "Millburn, I let you stay and watch them open the crate so you might be able to share something useful. I suggest you start talking or this is going to go even worse for you later. I promise you that!"

Sam grinned. He liked seeing Jerry get what was coming to him. He was a ne'er-do-well!

"Five years! That's how long I'd been hunting for this treasure," Jerry wailed. "I was in Tennessee for a reenactment and explored some old buildings that were about to go to auction. An old book from one of the lots caught my eye. It had the name *George Sweeney* written inside the cover. I bought it and started reading. Sure enough, it was the journal of George Wythe's grand-nephew.

"Sweeney had been only seventeen when Wythe was murdered. After he was acquitted in court, he just disappeared. By all historical accounts, no one knew where he'd gone."

"Tennessee!" shouted Derek.

Jerry glared at Derek but continued his story. "After Wythe's death, Jefferson's letter had arrived at the Wythe House. Sweeney stole it after the trial, intending to go back and retrieve the crate from its hiding spot in the garden.

"But time passed. As he grew old, he realized what a great man his uncle had been. In his regret, Sweeney decided to leave the Declaration copy in its place. So he returned to Richmond and hid the letter he'd stolen under the church. I think he decided that if someone found it after he died, no one could give him any more trouble.

"But how did you know something was under the church?" asked Sam.

Jerry sighed. "He left a series of clues in his journal and around his home in Tennessee that pointed to Church Hill. I finally found the last of them next to Wythe's grave at St. John's. That's when you meddling kids entered the picture and stole the letter before I was able to find it." He slumped his shoulders down and lowered his head, fully defeated now that he'd exposed his story.

"Wow," whistled Derek.

"That's quite a story," said Professor Evanshade. "Thank you for the explanation. It will be quite helpful in our research."

"But why didn't you just tell someone?" asked Caitlin. "Then you could have found the Declaration and not have almost killed us and gone to jail?"

"I think a lot of people should have told someone more than they did," Dad chimed in.

Jerry raised his head and stared at Caitlin with disgust. "Do you have any idea how much that document is worth on the black market?

"Fifty bucks?" asked Derek.

"Actually, this document could be virtually priceless," said Professor Evanshade.

"And it should have been mine!" Jerry exclaimed.

"It belongs in a museum," shouted Caitlin. "Not in your greedy clutches. You're supposed to be a historian, Mr. Patrick Henry. You should be ashamed of yourself."

"Nah," added Sam. "He's not a historian – just an actor."

"Well the show's over, Jerry!" shouted Derek. Everyone laughed, except for Jerry, who just glared at them.

SEVENTEEN

THE SURPRISE

"B eep! Beep! Beep!" The alarm clock rang out across the room.

"Sam! Turn it off," groaned Derek, barely lifting his head from the pillow.

"Too tired," said Sam, not wanting to move either.

It had been a long weekend. The boys had used up so much energy with the excitement in Williamsburg, they both wanted to sleep for a week. But Monday was here. School didn't care if they'd spent their weekend hunting for treasure from the American Revolution or playing video games on the couch.

After studying the early Declaration with Professor Evanshade back in Williamsburg, Mom and Dad had invited Caitlin and her parents over to Aunt Karen's for a late dinner. Everyone was still buzzing with enthusiasm from the events at the Wythe House.

Amidst the excitement, all three of the kids gave major apologies to their parents for being so deceptive. Dad was disappointed that they hadn't told him what was going on, especially after what had happened in the woods over the summer.

That time, Derek almost bit the dust when he was trapped in the cave with the lost coins. This time, they nearly had to spend the night locked in the basement of the Wythe House. Who knows what could have happened to them if Jerry had caught them again in the gardens?

Sam also agreed that he should have told Mrs. H as well as Mom and Dad about Jerry grabbing him at St. John's Church in the first place.

Sam turned off the alarm and sat up in his bed. He thought some more about what they'd found. It was incredible to know that the crate had been buried behind the house for all those years. It gave him the chills to think that Thomas Jefferson had written the words on that old paper. He felt a tiny bit bad that Jerry had worked so hard to find the clues that led him to St. John's Church, only to have the prize taken away.

Sam knew what it felt like to be hot on the trail of a mystery. It was easy to get carried away. But Jerry crossed the line. He wasn't trying to find a piece of history for good. He just wanted it for himself. Sam knew that Professor Evanshade would make sure the Declaration would be treasured. Maybe it would be displayed in Washington, D.C. near the Declaration's final version.

*　*　*

SOON, the boys were stepping off the school bus and heading toward their classrooms.

"Hey!" a voice called as someone bumped into Sam in the hallway. He turned and saw Caitlin next to him. He smiled and was surprised to feel happy to see her.

"Hey to you," he answered. "I can't believe we're back at school."

"I know! It's going to seem so *boring* after everything in Williamsburg."

Wait, Caitlin thought school was going to be boring? Sam didn't remember ever hearing her say that before. Usually she just acted like she knew everything and rubbed it in his face.

He had to admit, it had been fun having her along on the adventure. And it didn't hurt that she was so smart. It actually came in handy for a change! Maybe being friends with a girl wasn't so bad after all.

"What do you think is going to happen to Jerry?" asked Caitlin. "Do you think he's going to jail?"

"I don't know. Technically he didn't really steal anything, even though he tried to." Sam thought about what laws Jerry might have actually broken. "But he did grab me at the church. Then he kidnapped us and locked us in the basement."

"Right. Plus he resisted arrest when he tried to run away from the police officer," added Caitlin. "I'll bet that he won't be playing Patrick Henry at St. John's Church or in Colonial Williamsburg anymore."

"Maybe they have reenactments in prison!" suggested Sam.

Caitlin laughed. It was a genuine laugh, not just a pretend one.

"Sam?"

"Yeah?"

"Thank you for including me in your mystery. It was really fun."

"Well, you kind of invited yourself to Williamsburg," Sam replied.

Caitlin looked down. Sam wondered if he had embarrassed her. He thought about what she said and realized that she was actually trying to be nice to him.

He looked back at her. "I'm just kidding. It was fun to have you along. You were a big help."

"Really?" she beamed.

"Absolutely. Derek and I would have never known all that stuff about Sweeney or George Wythe without your research."

It was true. He never would have imagined it, but they made a good team.

"Friends?" she asked, holding her hand up. Did girls give high-fives? Apparently so. He slapped her open palm and grinned as they headed into their classroom.

Sam sat down in his seat and pulled out his notebook.

Billy Maxwell hustled through the doorway and looked up at the clock. "Yes! I'm early!" he shouted. He sank down on one knee and gave three big fist pumps.

He stood up, looked over at Sam, and nodded. "So Jackson, did you ever figure anything else out about those letters? Did you track down the Sharpie?"

Sam laughed. Some things hadn't changed a bit. "Actually, yes, Billy. It was a busy weekend. I'll tell you about it at recess."

After the pledge and announcements, Mrs. H stood up at the front of the room and got everyone's attention. "Our next chapter in our history unit, children, will be about the Civil War. But before we leave the American Revolution behind, who would like to share some of what they remember? It can be from our reading, the field trip, or something else that you learned on your own."

Caitlin's hand shot up with her typical sense of urgency. Hmm, thought Sam, maybe things hadn't changed as much as he thought. What was the expression Dad always used? "It's hard to teach an old dog new tricks"? Well, it had been fun while it lasted.

"Yes, Caitlin. What was most memorable for you?" said Mrs. H.

Sam braced himself for her inevitable showoff.

"Actually Mrs. H, I wanted to say that Sam had the most amazing adventure after our field trip. I'd really love for him to tell us all about it!"

Sam did a double-take, practically falling out of his chair. What had she just said?

Caitlin smiled and nodded to him, but he just sat there dumbfounded.

"Is that right?" Mrs. H said, more than a little surprised herself. "Well, Sam, why don't you tell us about it? It sounds exciting."

"Go Jackson! Go Jackson!" sang Billy from behind him.

"Well," gulped Sam, pulling his thoughts together. "It all started on our field trip when I really had to pee…"

The class burst out laughing.

Caitlin giggled and punched him in the shoulder. She gave him a serious smile and mouthed "Stop it!"

Sam turned around and saw that every eye was on him. He gathered his courage, picturing what Derek would say in a situation like this. Probably something outrageous. Hmm, maybe that wasn't such a good idea.

"Actually, Caitlin was a big part of things, too. And my brother Derek. It was kind of like Patrick Henry said."

"What do you mean, Sam?" asked Mrs. H.

"Well, for a while, we thought we were going to find death. But in the end, we found liberty."

He turned to Caitlin and motioned for her to tell the rest of the story. She was better at these kinds of things than he was anyhow.

"Are you sure?" she whispered.

Sam nodded.

Caitlin smiled. She sprang from her desk and marched to the front room.

Sam could tell this was going to take a while. But for once, he didn't mind.

GHOSTS OF BELLE ISLE

THE VIRGINIA MYSTERIES BOOK 3

Legend says that the haunting lights over the rapids on the James River at night are the ghosts of long-dead soldiers still fighting the Civil War. Just past the water lies historic Belle Isle, the former Union soldier prisoner-of-war camp, now a city park filled with crumbling ruins and dark wooded trails. When brothers Sam and Derek explore the island and local monuments to Richmond's past on the 150th anniversary of the Civil War with their friend Caitlin, some ghosts may be more alive than they expected! Join the adventure as the kids face their fears and a confederate biker gang led by the notorious Mad Dog DeWitt.

ACKNOWLEDGMENTS

Part of the fun in writing these books is getting to know the location and staff at places like St. John's Church. Sarah, Amy, Ray, and the whole team have been a pleasure to work with in our shared love of one of Richmond's most historic buildings. While I hadn't been in the church basement at writing, I've since had a peek, and my imagination wasn't far off. If you haven't been to one of the regular Liberty reenactments at St. John's, I strongly recommend it!

Thank you too to the folks at Colonial Williamsburg: Bob, Karen, and Brian, for all their support of all my books and visits. George Wythe was someone I'd never heard of growing up in New Jersey, but when I found the connection between St. John's and Williamsburg, it seemed like a perfect storyline. Be sure to visit his grave at

St. John's and the Wythe House in Williamsburg and see his solar microscope. Just keep a lookout for Jerry...

My family has been ever patient and supportive as I launched into a writing career without warning. My wife, Mary, and sons, Matthew, Josh, and Aaron, have endured many hours of Dad being holed up in his office working on "the book." The boys unknowingly provide a constant supply of material through their daily banter that helps bring Sam and Derek alive on the page. I also greatly enjoyed adding Caitlin as a main character. After hearing from many girls who enjoyed the first book, I realized something important was missing!

Thank you also to all my family and friends who have lent support and time in the process, especially Robin, Ryan, Libby, Ali, Julie, Jenni, James River Writers and Bettie Weaver Elementary. Thanks to Dane for the great cover, Melissa Rose for her interior illustrations, and Janie Lector for her polish.

Finally, thank you to my readers, young and old, who have shared their joy and kind words over the last few months. It means more than you know.

ALSO BY STEVEN K. SMITH

The Virginia Mysteries:

Summer of the Woods

Mystery on Church Hill

Ghosts of Belle Isle

Secret of the Staircase

Midnight at the Mansion

Shadows at Jamestown

Spies at Mount Vernon

Escape from Monticello

Brother Wars:

Brother Wars

Cabin Eleven

The Big Apple

Final Kingdom:

The Missing

The Recruit (Spring 2020)

ABOUT THE AUTHOR

Steven K. Smith is the author of *The Virginia Mysteries*, *Brother Wars*, and *Final Kingdom* series for middle grade readers. He lives with his wife, three young sons, and a golden retriever in Richmond, Virginia.

For more information, visit:

www.stevenksmith.net

steve@myboys3.com

CHAT

MYBOYS3 PRESS SUPPORTS CHAT

Sam, Derek, and Caitlin aren't the only kids who crave adventure. Whether near woods in the country or amidst tall buildings and the busy urban streets of a city, every child needs exciting ways to explore his or her imagination, excel at learning and have fun.

A portion of the proceeds from *The Virginia Mysteries* series will be donated to the great work of **CHAT (Church Hill Activities & Tutoring)**. CHAT is a non-profit group that works with kids in the Church Hill neighborhood of inner-city Richmond, Virginia.

To learn more about CHAT, including opportunities to volunteer or contribute financially, visit **www. chatrichmond.org.**

DID YOU ENJOY MYSTERY ON CHURCH HILL?

WOULD YOU ... REVIEW?

Online reviews are crucial for indie authors like me. They help bring credibility and make books more discoverable by new readers. No matter where you purchased your book, if you could take a few moments and give an honest review at one of the following websites, I'd be so grateful.

Amazon.com
BarnesandNoble.com
Goodreads.com

Thank you and thanks for reading!

Steve

CPSIA information can be obtained
at www.ICGtesting.com
Printed in the USA
BVHW070836070720
583008BV00005B/200

9 780986 147364